Track Down Amazon

A Brad Jacobs Thriller

Book 3

SCOTT CONRAD

PUBLISHED BY:
Scott Conrad

2nd Edition © May 2018

Copyright © 2016 - 2019
All rights reserved.

A Brad Jacobs Thriller Series by Scott Conrad:

TRACK DOWN AFRICA – BOOK 1

TRACK DOWN ALASKA – BOOK 2

TRACK DOWN AMAZON – BOOK 3

TRACK DOWN IRAQ – BOOK 4

TRACK DOWN BORNEO – BOOK 5

TRACK DOWN EL SALVADOR – BOOK 6

TRACK DOWN WYOMING – BOOK 7

Visit the author at: ScottConradBooks.com

"There are only two kinds of people that understand Marines: Marines and the enemy. Everyone else has a second-hand opinion."

Gen. William Thornson, U.S. Army

Table of Contents

Prologue

He splashed to a dead stop, his feet tangled in the submerged roots of yet another mangrove tree. He was wet, filthy and out of breath, and he was exhausted. Listening to the sounds of the swamp and its creatures around him, he could no longer hear any sounds of pursuing humans, and for that he felt profoundly grateful.

Having to run through the damned swamps was bad enough with its freaking carnivorous fish and various venomous, fanged, and toothed critters without insane men with guns chasing him. Delroy was not as outdoorsy as his brother, a career Marine, and he sure as hell didn't relish wading around in this dismal swamp. Frankly, the place scared the shit out of him.

Damned roots and "gotcha" vines seemed almost alive, grasping at him every step of the way, and when they weren't clutching at him, he was up to his ass in either alligators (he'd read somewhere that the creatures in the Amazon were Black Caimans but the bastards looked like alligators to him) or quicksand.

As if the critters weren't enough, Rodolfo Abimael Guzmán and his Senderistas wanted him ... and he knew very well what a bloodthirsty pack of savages they were. Guzmán was the grandson of the first leader of the Shining Path and head of the splinter group in Iquitos.

Delroy shuddered at the memories of the horrendous ritual murders and executions he observed while undercover in Iquitos. Even though he understood that his mission was truly vital in the most literal sense, his courage had faltered more than once during the last year. He had stayed, enduring the night sweats and the incredible fear, until twenty-four hours ago when his cover had been blown by a civilian who had known Delroy and his brother since their childhood.

Guzman himself had gone into a rage, sending his inner cadre after him with instructions to catch Delroy and bring him back and not to return without him on pain of death. It was unclear to Delroy whether he was to be brought back dead or alive or if Guzman didn't care.

Delroy hadn't waited around to find out. He escaped into the swamps north of Iquitos seconds ahead of the cadre and he had barely managed to stay ahead of them ... so far. He couldn't hear them any longer, and he assumed he had finally managed to elude them. He was wrong.

Chapter 1

Cabo San Lucas

Retrospective

DAY 0

He ran his fingers through his short, military style buzz cut and then bent over his desk and rested his head in his hands. The mission in Alaska had cost him a trusted friend, a Marine brother, and Tom Riggins' death hit him hard. "Combat losses" had always been hard on Brad, but losing someone on a civilian mission felt somehow worse, despite the personal nature of the job.

The light plane Pete had been flying was reported as missing. Pete Sabrowski was a brother, and brothers, especially Marine brothers, put their lives on the line for each other because that bond is as strong as blood. They had all known the risks when they found out about The Order, but not one of them had been willing to back down. Tom paid the ultimate price, and he would be missed. Brad sighed, accepting the loss and the responsibility.

He sat down in his desk chair and leaned back, staring at the ceiling. The penetrating cold of the Arctic was still with him. He felt as if he'd never be warm again, even though he was back in his Texas home.

Suddenly, he wanted to be someplace warm and sunny, someplace where he could enjoy tropical drinks and the coldest thing he'd have to worry about would be the condensation on the outside of a beer. Someplace with palm trees, warm breezes, and attractive women in tiny swimsuits.

The front door opened and Jessica strode in, arm in arm with Charlie. After many long conversations she finally understood his actions in Alaska and realized he really had feelings for her. They were rarely apart since the team had returned, and they were obviously in love. Brad made a spontaneous decision.

"Hi Jess! How would you two like to go to Cabo with me?"

"Cabo San Lucas?" she asked eagerly, delight clear on her face.

Brad chuckled. "Do you know of another Cabo?"

Hacienda Beach Club

Brad Jacobs lay back in the lounge chair, soaking up the warm rays of the sun as he took a sip of the icy brew that one of the pool waitresses had just delivered. The six-foot-two-inch blonde's green eyes remained hidden by the same Oakley sunglasses he had worn in Alaska so recently, which seemed just as well because he was enjoying the many delightful women who were basking in the sun around the pool and didn't want them to know he was doing so.

Whatever it was that made women wear such skimpy swimsuits in Mexico, he approved of it. His eyes shifted over to where his cousin Jessica was sitting in Charlie Dawkins' lap and grimaced. Well, mostly he liked it. He liked Charlie, and what was more he trusted the State Department special agent, but the idea of his gorgeous treasure-hunting cousin making the beast with two backs with the man still left him queasy.

It was hard to watch the cousin he had known since she was "knee high to a grasshopper" strutting around in a tiny bikini and climbing all over Dawkins. Fortunately, there were several distractions lolling around the pool to take his mind off Jessica.

One such distraction was wending her way towards the pool area at that very moment. She knew damned well every man near the pool was watching her, and it looked obvious that she was enjoying the attention. "Jesus," Brad heard Charlie say. "That bikini is made out of Band-Aids and dental floss!"

There was the sound of a playful slap and Jessica's low voice saying, "Put your eyes back in your head, Charlie Dawkins." Brad grinned and then turned his attention back to the slender redhead.

She was tall and lithe, with amazingly long legs and high, firm breasts. The bikini she wore was in fact incredibly tiny, concealing only enough of her to keep from being arrested. Once she had selected a lounge chair near Brad's, she slid her large sunglasses down her nose and gave him an appraising glance that sent tingles all the way down to his toes. She had luminous jade-green eyes and fabulously long lashes. Her mouth curved into a smile that promised everything.

"You should take a picture, sailor, it would last longer." Her voice was silky, sultry even.

"If I had a camera I would," Brad said, unabashed. "But I should warn you ... never call a Marine a sailor."

"You're a Marine?"

"Excuse me, retired Marine," he said lightly.

She stood up from the chair she had just sat down in and walked towards him. Brad was not the only person by the pool who watched her walk in his direction; the play of muscles in her trim body as she moved was mesmerizing.

Brad had always been an old-school gentleman around the fairer sex, but as he tried to stand up to meet her he realized too late that he was about to be embarrassed and had to grab a towel from his chair to hide his perfectly normal reaction to this Delilah. His face turned beet-red, but she extended her hand to him.

"Once a Marine, always a Marine," she said. Her hand was soft in his and the physiological manifestation of his gender assumed an even more embarrassing prominence, causing him to become tongue-tied. The woman's eyes cut down to the towel and lingered there, but Brad was saved by a peal of laughter from Jessica, who appeared totally delighted by his discomfort.

Jessica stood up and walked over to the two, her own hand extended. "I don't think I've ever seen my cousin struck dumb before and I'd love to shake the hand of the woman who managed it!"

The redhead turned and smiled warmly at Jessica. The handshake turned to an exuberant hug, and the two laughed uproariously.

"Vicky Chance," the redhead said, still smiling.

"Jessica Paul," Jess said. "The Marine standing here impersonating a beet is my cousin Brad Jacobs, and he was not only a Marine, he was something of a legend in Force Recon."

Vicky turned and gazed at Brad with even more genuine interest on her pretty face. She offered her hand again, and Brad took it, the towel in his free hand forgotten.

"2nd Marines," she said. Her grip was firm and strong. "When did you get out? I spent eight years there, and if you've been at Lejeune in the last five or six years we've probably walked right past each other."

Brad finally regained control of his tongue. "I got out six years ago." His mouth was dry as hell and he felt awkward, like a teenager about to ask a girl out for the first time. It was Charlie who got him off the hook.

"Cerveza for everybody!" Charlie called out. He ordered Coronas for all of them and the pool waitress brought the icy bottles out on a round tray she carried the way carhops had in the olden days at drive-in restaurants.

There was a comfortable silence as the four of them took their first sips of the icy brews. Brad sensed a very definite spark of some kind between himself and Vicky Chance, and it was much deeper than their shared experience as Marines. The closest he could come to describing the connection was chemistry, a catch-all term that laymen used to describe what a psychologist would call infatuation.

After they finished their beer, Jessica elbowed Charlie, who, in her opinion, was paying entirely too much attention to Vicky's bikini, and the two of them gave a lame excuse about going back to the residence Brad had booked to change before going sightseeing. They didn't fool either Brad or Vicky.

Vicky

Brad donned a brightly colored guayabera shirt and Vicky had thrown on a see-through cover-up that looked as exciting as the swimsuit beneath it, and the two of them wandered down to the Hacienda Cocina & Cantina terrace for a late afternoon snack. The terrace seemed quieter than the pool area, and it was easier to talk without the distractions at the pool. Brad was no longer thinking about Jessica and what she might be doing; his attention was focused on the spectacular redhead.

"So you were with Force Recon?" Vicky said, her hand toying with the water glass the waitress had placed in front of her when they sat down.

Brad opened his mouth to speak but stopped as the waitress set a coffee cup in front of him and filled it from a stainless carafe. He never even looked at her; he was totally absorbed in Vicky.

"Yes, I was with Force Recon for ten years."

"Those boys were a pretty tight-knit group," Vicky observed, sipping at her water glass.

Brad watched her upper lip curve over the rim of the glass in what was as much a caress as it was a touch. He had to shake his head and clear it before he could resume their conversation.

Easy buddy… This one's dynamite.

"Like brothers," Brad agreed. He cocked his head to one side. "So what did the Crotch have you doing?" (A popular, if irreverent, definition of the acronym USMC is Uncle Sam's Moldy Crotch. The definition is safe enough to share with other Marines, but it has been known to start fistfights when used by lesser beings.)

"Oh, nothing exciting," she said dismissively, "at least nothing like you were doing. I was with the 2nd Law Enforcement Battalion."

14

Brad was ready to ask her what she did as an M.P. when he felt her hand on his thigh. "How do you feel about moonlight swims?" she asked in a sultry voice that sent shivers up his spine. He could only nod his head. "Then meet me on the beach in an hour... I've promised to phone home this afternoon and I haven't yet."

Brad watched, stupefied, as she walked away from their table. He wasn't the only one; men all around the restaurant noticed her too. More than one of them had to deal with frosty stares from their own female companions.

As he walked back to his room, it occurred to him that she had been a little evasive regarding her work in the Corps, but the memory of how she looked in her bikini soon crushed any curiosity he might have had about her military occupational specialty.

Moonlight

If anything, the swimsuit she wore on the beach that night looked even smaller than the one she had worn to the pool that afternoon. She grabbed his hand and tugged him into the crashing waves until they were waist deep, and then she turned to face him.

A master wave shoved her into his arms and their lips met, and Brad, never a fast mover when it came to women, didn't want to let her go. The sound of the waves and the extraordinary bundle of woman in his arms kept him from seeing Jessica and Charlie on the beach spying on them.

Chapter 2

Grim News

Mason

Day 1, 1807 Hours Local Time

Mason Ving grew up in a ghetto in New Orleans and his mother passed away when he was just twelve years old. He was the oldest of three brothers, and he had taken a paper route to help his father put food on the table. He'd joined the Marine Corps when he reached his eighteenth birthday to escape the poverty of the ghetto and to help support his family.

That had been a hell of a long time ago. He'd never dreamed that someday he would own his own home in a nice neighborhood in Fort Worth, Texas, much less be married to the woman of his dreams and have two great kids of his own.

Mason's retirement pay, augmented by the generous income provided by his work with his closest friend, Brad Jacobs, enabled him to keep his father in a local nursing home. Both of his brothers had also joined the Corps: one was still on active duty and the other had done a single tour, gone back to college on the G.I. Bill, and then joined the ranks of the Drug Enforcement Administration as a Special Agent. His income also enabled him to keep his wife and his own two children in comfortable style in a well-to-do suburb of Fort Worth.

Ving was a proud and arrogant man, but when he was at home with his beautiful wife and children, he felt humbled by his good fortune. As a matter of fact, his closest friends would have hardly recognized him at home; his wife Willona quietly ruled the house and the two children, Jordan and Nathaniel.

Willona had been the one who squirreled away a portion of their money every month, eking it out of their tight budget on a regular basis. She had taken college level classes everywhere they had been stationed, and she learned to invest the money wisely. She never told Mason what she did with the money and he never asked; he was far too busy keeping himself alive in the hellholes the Corps had sent him to.

One of her professors put her on to a couple of stocks that really turned out to be winners, Microsoft and Oracle. Mason had been truly astonished to find out when he retired that the expensive house in Fort Worth was not only within his price range but that he could pay cash for it. He was further astounded when Willona presented him with a brand new Ford Expedition when they moved in, as well as a new Ford Explorer for herself.

Willona had fantastic taste in furnishings and over the years managed to acquire an impressive collection. After moving into the new house, she'd used her acumen to start a rather profitable side business buying and selling antiques. The four-bedroom Colonial in Fort Worth quickly filled up with fine furnishings, and Mason had moved his trophies and mementos to a room he'd added onto the back of the garage. He called it his office, but it was also where he stored his personal weapons.

Mason and the kids had just sat down at the table, and Willona had just brought out a platter of crispy fried bacon and a tray of lettuce, tomatoes, and bread, when the doorbell rang. Mason ignored it; few things on Earth could distract him from his bacon. Willona, exasperated and amused at the same time, went to answer the doorbell.

"Bacon!" Mason growled gleefully as he dug into the pile on the platter. Jordan and Nathaniel laughed at his antics; his love of bacon was familiar and funny to them, though Nathaniel shared his dad's love of the breakfast meat.

"Mason," Willona called from the foyer.

"What is it, woman? Don't you realize I'm 'baconating'?" he asked. The kids cracked up, their playful laughter filling the formal dining room.

"Mason," Willona said, walking into the room, "Come here!"

Mason looked up at Willona's stricken face and immediately his demeanor changed. She had been smiling only moments before, but she looked fearful now. Whatever the problem was, it was serious. He glanced down the table at his son. "Don't mess with my bacon, son," he said mock seriously. Whatever was wrong, he wouldn't let it touch his children.

Mason Ving, all 275 pounds of him, strode through the dining room and into the foyer like the six-foot bruiser he was. His normally friendly brown eyes were in deadly focus and his eyebrows were shaped into a fierce scowl. His bald pate shone in the bright light of the foyer, the chandelier there had been one of Willona's most prized acquisitions.

He marched over to where his wife stood with a solemn-faced man who possessed the look of a mid-level government bureaucrat from one of the alphabet agencies—C.I.A., F.B.I., I.C.E. or maybe Homeland Security. He wasn't sure.

"Mason," Willona said, "It's Delroy."

Ving felt as if a sledgehammer had hit him in the chest. Delroy Ving was the brother who joined the D.E.A., and Ving knew that he was working undercover somewhere in South America, but he didn't know the specifics of his brother's assignment.

His eyes went to the man in the expensive suit. "What's wrong? What's happened to my brother?"

"Mr. Ving, I'm Chance Sutton with the D.E.A. and I work with Delroy. Is there somewhere we can talk?" Sutton glanced nervously at Willona and then back at Mason. "We really need to do this in private, and then you can choose what to discuss with your wife afterwards. I'm truly taking a chance by even being here."

Mason studied the man closely. He didn't like the idea of excluding Willona, but he realized the D.E.A. guy was scared of something, so he motioned for the man to follow him. Mason gave Willona a reassuring kiss and a knowing glance, letting her know subliminally that he would tell her everything afterwards.

She understood her husband all too well, and she kept her face calm. "Do you want me to bring you a pot of coffee?"

"No baby," Ving said, "I'll make a fresh pot in the office." He led the way through the kitchen to the back door and out to the office behind the garage with Sutton in tow.

He unlocked the office door with a high tech secure key from his dog tag chain and held the door open for the D.E.A. man. "Sit," he said not unkindly to the bureaucrat as he pointed at a green leather-covered wingback chair in front of his polished mahogany desk. Even his private office hadn't escaped Willona's attention, and it looked more as if it belonged in a law firm than it did to the battle-scarred Mason Ving.

Mason stepped over to a mahogany credenza that matched the desk and prepared a pot of coffee. While it was brewing, he opened a door in the center of the credenza and withdrew two china mugs and a plate with sugar and creamer packets and set them on top of the cabinet. His mind was racing as he performed his tasks perfunctorily, and by the time the coffee was ready, he had prepared himself for the worst.

He set the tray with the steaming mugs atop his desk and set a spoon next to the tray before sitting down in his own desk chair, which was elevated about four inches higher than the wingback. The height difference meant that Mason was looking down at his visitor and Sutton had to look up to talk to him. It was a subtle psychological toy, and one that Ving used to his advantage on many occasions.

"Give it to me without the window dressing," he said, staring down at Sutton. "What's happened to Delroy?"

"Mr. Ving—" Sutton started.

Ving raised his hand for Sutton to stop. "Belay the mister shit, just call me Ving."

"Alright, Ving, as far as we know, Delroy is still alive."

"Who is 'we'?" Ving asked, his voice filled with ice.

"As I said, I'm with the D.E.A."

"Yeah, I got that, but who is 'we'? And what the hell does 'as far as we know' mean? Are you his supervisor, his department head? Just who the hell are you?" Ving's concern about his brother was making him impatient, and he understood he would have to stay calm or this feather merchant was not going to tell him anything at all.

"Ving, I'm not Delroy's supervisor, I'm just one of the field agents… I'm a friend. The reason I'm here is that Delroy is my friend and the agency is hanging him out to dry."

Delroy Situation

Delroy Ving was a special agent for the Justice Department's Drug Enforcement Administration

(DEA), under special assignment to the secretary of state to assist both D.E.A. agents and their law enforcement counterparts in Peru, specifically in the Amazon basin, headwaters of the Amazon River.

His mission was to gather tactical and strategic intelligence on the current cocaine drug trafficking from cultivation to distribution. The information was vital to the U.S. Government for use in making decisions on resource allocation and deployment and on immediate enforcement actions.

Delroy's mission had gone south, and he had been taken prisoner in the jungle around Iquitos, Peru by members of a local unit of the Shining Path, a Maoist guerrilla group led by Rodolfo Abimael Guzmán. One of Guzmán's lieutenants, a man the D.E.A. previously identified as Rafael Fernandez, contacted the D.E.A. office in Iquitos via Delroy's satellite phone and demanded a ransom for Delroy's safe return. The supervisory special agent

(SSA) bumped the demand upstairs after negotiating a seven-day 'waiting period' to acquire the two million dollars in cash the lieutenant had specified.

An indignant department head working at the Southern Cone Desk in D.E.A. headquarters had immediately rebuffed the SSA, stating that the U.S. maintained a policy of not negotiating with terrorists, and ordered a blackout on all other communications or actions concerning one Delroy Ving. The SSA argued rather weakly with the department head and then meekly agreed to do as he was ordered.

"Ving, it's true we don't negotiate with terrorists, but this is the first time in my career that I'm aware of the Agency just keeping a lid on such a circumstance. Jesus, when something like this happens they call in Delta Force or Special Forces or the Rangers and those guys come in and kick the shit out of whoever is fucking with us."

"Or Force Recon," Ving said thoughtfully. He had been on a few clandestine operations himself, though he'd been utilized in Africa and the Middle East. The Southern Cone required a whole different set of language and cultural skills, and the Force Recon guys at Pendleton handled that area of operations. The assignments came out of Joint Special Operations Command (JSOC) in Dam Neck, Virginia.

Ving sipped at his coffee, giving himself a chance to think, reviewing what he remembered about the Shining Path movement. He knew it was a Maoist guerrilla insurgent group in Peru and that when it first appeared in Peru, in 1980, its goal was to replace what it perceived as "bourgeois democracy" with "New Democracy". The Shining Path or Sendero Luminoso movement felt it could create a dictatorship of the proletariat, induce a cultural revolution, and ultimately provide the catalyst for a world revolution resulting in pure communism.

Their leaders claimed that the existing socialist governments were revisionist and they claimed to have taken the mantle of leadership of the world communist movement. The Shining Path's methods and ideology had been copied by other Maoist insurgent groups and other revolutionary internationalist movement-related parties.

Widely condemned for its brutality against peasants, popularly elected officials, trade union organizers and the general civilian population, the Shining Path had been classified as a terrorist organization by the U.S., the European Union, Canada, and the Peruvian government. After the capture of Abimael Guzmán (cousin to Rodolfo) in 1992, the Shining Path almost faded away, but splinter groups and offshoots of the Shining Path movement transitioned to very efficient cocaine-smuggling operations, as well as human trafficking organizations. From what Ving had read, the left-wing rebels still maintained three hundred fifty odd members and roughly eighty fighters.

The Shining Path guerillas conducted a bloody insurrection in Peru from 1980 onwards. After their leader, the man known as Comrade Artemio, had been captured in 2012, President Ollanta Humala announced the Shining Path had been defeated and called off the Peruvian Army. According to the reports Ving read, the remnants were supposed to be centered on the Apurimac-Ene and the Mantaro River Valley, an area most often referred to by its Spanish acronym, VRAEM. He had not been aware of any splinter groups as far north as Iquitos.

Frustrated, Ving's temper flared as he glowered at Sutton. "There's something you ain't tellin' me and I'm just about to tear you a new one unless you come clean." The D.E.A. operative was clearly scared, and his hand went to the opening of his suit coat, but Ving had the jump on him. His own hand came out from beneath the desk and it held a massive custom M-1911 with a brown parkerized finish, Pachmayr grips, and adjustable micro sights with tritium dots on the blade and sight aperture. He set the big automatic on the desk within reach of his outstretched hand, almost daring the D.E.A. man to go for his own weapon.

Sutton shrugged and then heaved a deep sigh. "Look man, I came here to help my friend, not start a fight."

Ving was hot. "The only thing I give a rat's ass about is the truth, Sutton. What the fuck is goin' on with the D.E.A. down in that hellhole that you're not tellin' me?"

Sutton stared down at his shoes. "I don't think this op is sanctioned." He waited as if he fully expected Ving to shoot him.

"Not sanctioned?" Ving asked, his voice as cold as death.

"I think this is something Renfroe, the Peru Ops Department head, dreamed up to get some brownie points or maybe a promotion. I hear the guy who runs the Southern Cone Desk is retiring."

"And you think now this Renfroe asshole is gonna leave my baby brother to the mercy of this Guzman character to keep from getting his ass in a crack and losing his shot at a promotion?"

The look on Sutton's face told Ving he was spot on in his assessment. He sat back in his desk chair, ignoring Sutton for a moment. The hollow feeling in the pit of his stomach was not going to go away until he found out more about Delroy. Hostage dealings with terrorists were generally a losing proposition, and he couldn't honestly assess Delroy's chances of still being alive at better than fifty/fifty.

The Shining Path's Senderistas were no longer a viable political entity, if indeed they ever had been. They were a ragtag collection of ruthless cutthroats, thieves, and kidnappers, and, if the truth were told, the U.S. State Department retained circumstantial evidence that they were deeply involved in human trafficking, mostly underage girls for the sex trade.

Delroy was a black man and a U.S. Federal agent. The Senderistas would not be inclined towards being nice to him. There was a slim chance that they might need the money bad enough to keep him alive to get the ransom, and Ving knew he had to give it a shot.

He sought Sutton's eyes, and when he made contact, he asked the question that had been bugging him since the man first told him Delroy's situation. "Why did you come to me, why didn't you stay in-house with the D.E.A.? Don't you have an internal affairs unit?"

Sutton met his gaze. "You're Delroy's brother, he idolizes you…"

"And?"

Sutton dropped his glance and stared at his lap. "We have an internal board of review. Renfroe is the acting chairman." His eyes rose to meet Ving's once more and his voice was clearer and more distinct. "I didn't take it before the review board because I believe Renfroe will shrug this off as unimportant. I'd get the rote answer—the U.S. doesn't negotiate with terrorists. The man doesn't give a shit about anything but covering his own ass and I believe he will leave Delroy swinging in the breeze. Whatever Renfroe has got going on down there, he doesn't want anyone to pay any attention to it."

The Big Guns

Day 1 2013 Hours Local Time

Ving remained in his garage office long after Sutton left. He removed a yellow legal pad from the top left drawer of the desk and then took a plain black ball-point pen that displayed "U.S.

Government" stamped on the side of it from the top center drawer. He clicked the top of the pen several times as he thought and then began to list everything he knew about the Shining Path movement on the top sheet, leaving at least three inches of space between each fact. When he was finished, he had seven sheets of paper.

He twisted around in his desk chair and booted up the PC on top of his desk and began to Google references to the facts on his pad. After adding two more yellow sheets to his growing pile and then filling them both up, he pulled up a detailed map of Peru on his flat screen computer monitor and zoomed in on Iquitos. With a click of his mouse, he changed the image on the screen from a cartographic map to an aerial photographic map. A detailed analysis of the area surrounding Iquitos gave him no sense of where the Senderistas might be hiding out; there simply was nothing, no structures of any kind visible in the aerial photographs.

There was little public information about Rodolfo Abimael Guzmán other than that he was a distant cousin of the philosophy professor Abimael Guzmán who originally founded the Shining Path movement. After two hours of intensive effort, Ving tossed his pen down on the desktop and rubbed his eyes.

He realized what he must do. Even though Brad Jacobs was his closest friend, he hadn't wanted to drag him into a mess like this, but Brad was like family and Delroy was blood. He had no choice. Ving reached for the telephone, pressing the speed dial number for Brad's satellite phone.

Willona would be pissed; he had just come back from Alaska. She would forgive him because she loved Delroy, too, but she would make Ving pay, no doubt about it.

Chapter 3

Mission: Go

Alert

Day 1 2327 Hours, Local Time

The raucous chirps from his satellite phone on the dresser in the bedroom stirred Brad from the relaxed state he was in following his evening romp with Vicky and brought him to an immediate state of alert. The satellite phone number had only been given to a very few people, and none of them would use it except in an emergency.

He padded naked across the deep pile carpet to the dresser and lifted the phone, then slipped into the adjoining room so as not to wake Vicky. It was Ving, and it was indeed an emergency. Brad listened quietly as Ving described Delroy's situation in terse, concise terms.

When Ving was through with his recitation, Brad took a single moment to evaluate the problem and make a decision. "Okay Ving, got a pen and paper handy?"

"Yeah," Ving said, reaching for the black pen he'd just put down and folding back a clean sheet of yellow legal paper on the pad.

"Good, write this down. Use the war chest credit card for all this." The war chest credit card was an American Express card with no limit, a card which Brad paid off religiously at the end of every month. Ving remained the only authorized user besides Brad.

"Alert Jared and Pete, pick them up, and get your asses to the airport. I'll call as soon as I'm off here and arrange a charter on a small jet."

"Since it's a charter, Brad, should we bring weapons?"

"No way, Ving. The Federales are inspecting everything, even private charters, coming into Cabo from the U.S. They're checking everything with a fine-toothed comb and as far as I can tell nothing is getting by them. We'll pick up weapons in Columbia... I know a guy. I'm hiring the charter because we don't have much time and I need to get you here ASAP. I also plan to use the same aircraft to get us all from here to Columbia."

"Columbia?" Ving repeated.

"Just do it, brother. I know you're hurting, Delroy is your baby brother and you're just not all there right now. Just remember, your family is my family, man, you're my brother." It was said without drama; the bond between the two former Marines was forged in combat and annealed in blood. There was nothing the two men would not do for each other.

Ving hung up as he was bid without further questions and Brad immediately dialed the home number of the owner of a charter jet company in Dallas he had used before on a moment's notice.

"Jeff, this is Brad."

The owner responded in a sleepy voice.

"Yeah, sorry to wake you, but how fast can you get wheels up in the G 280?"

Jeff sounded fully awake on the other end by this time and gave a short answer.

"Yeah, the 450 will do if the 280 isn't available. Wind up the rubber bands and get it out on the tarmac. Ving and a couple of others are en route now, should be there within the hour."

Jeff's response was short and sweet.

Brad laughed. "No, Jeff, no contraband, no weapons, just a hop to Cabo and then on to Cali a few hours later." Jeff said something and Brad laughed drily and hung up. He had a plan to formulate and at most three hours to get it done.

Planning

Brad started to knock on Jessica's door and then thought better of it. She was a grown woman and well over twenty-one, so he held no right to judge her on whom she might or might not take into her bed. He resolved the problem by calling her on her satellite phone.

"Jess, I need you to get up and get out here... We got a mission and I need some help in a hurry."

Jessica's laughter trilled over the phone. "I don't have to get up, Brad. Didn't you check my room? Charlie and I are out at the Cantina having a nightcap. We'll be there in a second." She disconnected, leaving Brad staring first at the sat phone in his hand and then at Jessica's bedroom door. He gave his head a wry shake... He had made assumptions based on facts not on evidence, a rookie mistake. If he wanted to get Delroy out of his predicament he would have to get his head in the game.

By the time the coffee he'd ordered from room service arrived, Brad had forced his mind back into the groove and sent Jessica and Charlie out to collect aviation charts for South America. The decision to include Charlie was easily made. He'd earned a little time off after his Alaska assignment, and Jessica appeared determined to take him along. Jess had proven herself to be one of the team over the last two missions, and Brad wasn't about to start second-guessing her at this point.

He sat down at the huge dining table in the three-bedroom residence with a mug of coffee and his sat phone and booted up his laptop. Waiting for Jess and Charlie, he analyzed the problem Ving had outlined for him.

Delroy had been taken captive by a splinter group from the Shining Path movement, a former Maoist organization that he understood was now far more involved in the drug trade than in politics. The drug lords of Peru and Ecuador had surged to the forefront of the trade once the Columbians had been battered into submission, and they were every bit as savage and ruthless as their predecessors … some said they were worse.

Brad was painfully aware that Delroy was probably already dead; the Senderistas were notorious for demanding ransom money and then failing to hold up their end of the bargain. Often as not they would show up at the designated rendezvous point with overwhelming force, leaving the payees with a dead body or nothing for their money and efforts. Unfortunately, failing to meet their demands usually resulted in the death, often ugly and painful, of the victim.

Brad had absolutely no intention of paying the ransom. He would make up a dummy bag with just enough cash salted across the top to fool the damned Senderistas and stall until the Shining Path headquarters in Iquitos could be located. Once they found where Delroy was being held, the team would take the site with a concentrated excess of force and wreak as much havoc on the small handful of Senderistas in the splinter group as his little band of outlaws was capable of—and their particular skill set made them capable of creating a great deal of havoc.

It wasn't a very imaginative plan, but it worked time and again for Force Recon teams seeking to confuse and demoralize a force of superior numbers. Under the circumstances, it would have to do; there wasn't time for anything more elaborate and there were no more resources in the area that he could count on.

The D.E.A. had decided to feed Delroy to the wolves; there would be no help from that quarter, according to Ving. On the positive side, Brad knew he had a superlative collection of some of the best shooters that Force Recon ever produced on his team.

Ving and Pete were regular artists with automatic weapons, and Jared remained legendary with his Barrett .50 sniper rifle. Jessica proved to be rock steady under fire, and Charlie appeared plenty smart, having acquitted himself well in the firefight at the cliffs in Alaska. Brad maintained no illusions about his own abilities; he had proven them time and again in hairy situations over the past twenty years.

With a very basic idea of a plan set in his head, Brad turned to his laptop. There was a retired Army warrant officer running an aviation leasing company out of Cali, Columbia that he needed to locate and talk with right away. CW5 Samuel Eggers had flown MH-6 Little Bird helicopters for the 160th Special Operations Aviation Regiment (SOAR), the Night Stalkers, in Afghanistan, and he enjoyed extracting Brad and Ving both from a number of very hairy situations over the years.

Marines were famous for their loyalty and allegiance to each other, but certain men in other branches were occasionally admitted into the bond of the brotherhood. Eggers was one of those special individuals. It only took a few minutes for Brad to locate the company website and get the listing.

Brad scanned through the website, getting a feel for Eggers' company. According to the site A & E Aviation, Eggers appeared to be partnered with a retired Marine lieutenant colonel named Richard Ackerman. This helicopter leasing company serviced oil fields and oil exploration teams in the Amazon Basin and maintained branch offices in Ecuador, Peru and Brazil.

Even though it happened to be late at night, there remained a switchboard operator to handle emergency calls. It took all of Brad's persuasive powers plus the promise of a premium charter to get her to pass him through to Eggers' personal phone.

Eggers recognized his voice immediately, even though he had been awakened from a sound sleep. "Brad! How the hell are you, buddy?"

"I'm great, Chief. How's retired life treating you?"

"I'm loving every minute of it, buddy, but to tell you the truth, sometimes I miss the regiment."

Brad laughed into the phone. "At least you're getting woken up at all hours of the day and night for other people's emergencies."

"True," Eggers said, chuckling. His tone suddenly changed. "Brad, you in some kind of trouble?"

"Not me, Chief, Ving."

"What's up with Ving?" The concern appeared evident in Eggers' voice. Ving had dragged him out of the flaming wreckage of a Little Bird once in the mountains north of Jalalabad. Ving and Brad had guarded the badly injured Eggers until a Medevac chopper could get to them.

A team of six AH-6 helicopters, the assault version of the MH-6 Little Bird, provided covering fire for the Medevac chopper and the men on the ground. The three of them spent most of a day in a rock-strewn stream behind a boulder waiting for their extraction. Ving and Brad had been decorated for the action and Eggers enjoyed being a blood brother ever since.

"It's not really Ving, Chief, it's his little brother Delroy. To make a long story short, he's a D.E.A. agent and he's been taken captive by a splinter group of the Shining Path in Iquitos. The D.E.A., for reasons we don't know for sure, are leaving him swinging in the wind."

"Fucking politicians!" Eggers' voice resonated bitter. "Tell me what you need, Brad."

Brad gave the man a rough outline of the mission and a sketchy list of his needs—including weapons.

Eggers didn't hesitate. "We don't normally handle ordnance requirements, but from time to time we do special favors for the 'company'." He was, of course, referring to the C.I.A. and its 'Wet Teams' operations. 'Wet Teams' handled situations and missions that could not be acknowledged by the State Department. "How long before you arrive?"

Brad glanced down at his chronograph and did a few mental calculations. "About twenty-four hours, give or take," he said. "Ving's on his way here and we'll be in the air as soon as we come up with a rough operations order and collect a little more intelligence."

"I'll go ahead and reach out to my contact. I'm thinking he's going to have everything you need in stock. You can give me a specific list of your requirements when you get here and we can pick them up."

"Any chance my guys can do a little hands-on shopping, Chief? They're the best in the business and sometimes they're a bit picky about their weapons."

"I'll have to check, Brad. He keeps his warehouse location a secret for obvious reasons, but I imagine he'll let you in if I vouch for you."

"Thanks Chief, I owe you."

"Anything you might have owed me was paid in full at Jalalabad, brother. Looking forward to seeing you again."

Respite

Brad found that he had done all he could do for the time being, but his work ethic demanded he do something concerned with the mission. It prevailed as a mindset that made him the superior warrior that he was. He sighed and brought up the satellite images of Iquitos and the surrounding areas once more.

There had to be something there that would spark his imagination, enable him to piece together some tidbit of intelligence he had missed. After several minutes studying the images, he reviewed all the information he possessed on the Shining Path and the splinter group in Iquitos, especially on Rodolfo Abimael Guzman.

After his third cup of coffee, his mind drifted back to Vicky despite his efforts to focus on Delroy Ving. Over the years he had been in several relationships. He never lacked for feminine companionship, but the Corps and his profession hadn't allowed for a serious relationship. Vicky was something different in his life.

First, she appeared drop dead gorgeous, which in itself seemed reason enough to dwell on her in his mind from time to time. Second, she looked to be some kind of an exhibitionist, which was not really a character trait that Brad sought in a woman friend, but Vicky seemed to make it a game and Brad felt secretly thrilled by it. Third, but by no means last, she was something of an enigma. He knew she had been in a law enforcement battalion, which in his mind translated to her being a military police officer, but whenever he asked her about it, she quickly changed the subject.

Even more curious, she deflected any questions about what she did for a living once she got out of the Corps. She did tell him she lived in Myrtle Beach, South Carolina with her mother, that her father died years before, and that she had no siblings. Vicky had attended Duke University and graduated with a degree in psychology. She appeared intelligent, well-read, witty, and, Brad had discovered to his pleasure, very passionate.

They become close, and she even spent the night in his room. No one ever penetrated his natural reserve so quickly or completely, and he felt more than a little surprised at the feelings she engendered in him. It seemed entirely out of character for him to be distracted when he was planning a mission.

Chapter 4

Vicky Chance

Arrival

Day 2, 0500 Hours Local Time

Big Pete Sabrowski was the first one off the charter jet, dwarfing the exit door. Oddly enough, the big bear of a man was an incredible pilot. He could fly anything that would stay in the air ... and that he could fit his big frame in.

Jared Smoot, the lanky, raw-boned Texan, was the next one down the fold-down stairs. If there existed a better sniper than Smoot Brad had never met him, and he was mean as a snake in a firefight.

Ving came last, and as soon as Brad caught sight of his face, he was worried about his friend's state of mind. Absolute faith in Ving was the foundation of their relationship, but the tiniest smidgen of doubt entered Brad's mind as he watched his closest friend debark from the jet. His heart rejected the idea out of hand, but Brad's tactician's mind considered the possibility that his old friend might have to sit this mission out.

Before he could take Ving on this mission, Brad would have to determine whether the man was too close to this one because the man whose life depended on them was Ving's baby brother.

Brad had driven the rental Suburban out onto the tarmac next to the private terminal. Cabo remained a very popular destination for the wealthy and famous, and there were several new Learjets and Gulfstreams parked by the building. There was also a gleaming new HondaJet, a model Pete had never seen before. Only Ving's low growl kept Pete moving towards Brad and the Suburban.

The tension among the three travelers appeared obvious as Brad drove the rental SUV back to the Hacienda Beach Club, and none of them spoke.

Brad decided that it was going to be necessary to break one of his strictest rules, and he tightened his grip on the steering wheel.

Facedown

Jessica welcomed the travelers in her typical exuberant fashion, wrapping her arms first around Pete and then Jared, giving them a big smack on the cheek. She hugged Ving, but the massive black man didn't even smile in response. Chuck simply stood there looking uncomfortable.

Brad gave Chuck a glance and said, "Start without us." He turned to Ving and motioned for his friend to follow him. Ving complied humorlessly. When they entered Brad's bedroom, Brad closed the door behind them and walked over to the carved wooden armoire that served to enclose a television set. It also contained a bottle of Russell's Reserve Rye Whiskey and a couple of real glass tumblers, as opposed to the wrapped plastic tumblers usually found in hotels.

Brad carried the bottle and glasses over to the king-sized bed and set them down on the bedside table before motioning for Ving to join him. The heavily muscled, bald black man moved expressionlessly to the bed and sat down; then he mutely accepted the tumblerful of rye that Brad poured for him and gulped it down in one swallow. Brad swallowed his own drink and poured another for both of them, making a show of capping the bottle and putting it away.

Ving swallowed the second drink and watched as Brad finished his own. "You've never permitted us a drink once we've been alerted for a mission," Ving said evenly. "Why now? Why just me?"

Brad kept the emotion off his face. "Because I have to know, brother. Is this mission too close to your heart? I'm afraid I'm going to have to bench you because you're so emotionally involved in this one.

I realize I'm risking the lives of the whole team by letting you make this decision yourself, but I owe you, brother. It's your call."

To his credit, Ving didn't answer right away. His face screwed up in a mask of concentration, and for an instant, Brad thought he might see the man cry for the first time ever. The cycle of emotions ravaged Ving's face, changing every fifteen seconds or so… Brad didn't time them. When Ving finally came to a decision, his face transitioned into his mission face and there was no trace of emotion in his voice. "I'm in, Brad."

There was no way Brad could keep the emotion out of his own voice, so he simply clapped the big man on his shoulder. He would take Ving at his word. It was a testament to the depth of the relationship between the two men. Brad no longer held any doubts. Ving would maintain.

The Interloper

Brad and Ving re-entered the great room and walked into an awkward situation. Vicky was standing near the table covered with Brad's maps and notes, and the computer map with Iquitos magnified was still on the screen of his open laptop.

Vicky was dressed in a skimpy swimsuit and sandals, having decided to come over and invade Brad's bed once more. Pete and Jared were staring at the redhead open-mouthed, and Charlie was loyally cuddled up to Jessica and trying desperately (and unsuccessfully) not to stare at the incredible expanse of tanned skin Vicky was showing. Jessica, totally self-confident, looked amused by the mens' reaction.

Brad was not concerned that the mission might be compromised, but he wasn't sure he felt comfortable with Vicky knowing what they were about to get up to. The sudden silence in the room was deafening.

Vicky had taken in the maps, the notes, the charts, and the photo of Rudolfo Abimael Guzman Brad had pulled up on split screen and superimposed over the Google Earth map of Iquitos at a single glance.

"Well, well," she said with a wry smile. Her eyes lingered on Ving, Pete, and Jared, recognizing them for the shooters they were just by the way they carried themselves and their demeanor. "If I was a suspicious woman I would just about have to believe that my newfound playmate has a hard-on for a chickenshit, child stealing, pedophile sonofabitch."

Everyone in the room did a double take. "Huh?" Brad was completely floored.

"Guzman," Vicky said, pointing at the photo on Brad's laptop. "Don't try to tell me you didn't know the guy was heavy into human trafficking. I've been hunting that bastard all over the Southern Cone. How the hell did you find him in—" she stared at the map again "—Iquitos, Peru?"

Brad stared at her open-mouthed, but it was Ving who spoke first.

"The only trafficking we know he's into is cocaine … and I've got a hard-on for him because he's kidnapped my brother. I'm gonna kill the sonofabitch."

"How the hell do you know about Guzman, Vicky?" Brad sputtered.

Vicky had the good grace to blush. "I haven't lied to you, Brad; I just haven't told you the whole truth about myself. I had no idea you were down here getting ready to set up a mission to go after Guzman. I did know about your hostage rescue business and your bounty hunting. I'm careful regarding who I associate with so I ran a background check on you before I invited you down to the beach the other night."

Jessica chuckled and both Vicky and Brad turned towards her. Chuck was red-faced and squirming next to her.

"Chuck and I saw you down at the beach," Jessica explained. "I was going to stay and watch, but Chuck here is kind of bashful." She draped her arm over Chuck's shoulders, and he turned an even brighter red than he had been a moment earlier.

"I hope I didn't embarrass your boyfriend," Vicky said wryly.

"Not at all. He turned his head when he saw you untie the top of your swimsuit." Jessica was enjoying Brad and Chuck's discomfort.

"What the hell do you mean you ran a background check on me?" Brad demanded.

"I told you I haven't told you everything about me," Vicky said calmly. "I was a CWO-4 in the Marine Corps, and I was a C.I.D. special agent assigned to the 2nd Law Enforcement Battalion at Lejeune. When I got out, I applied for a job as a special agent with Immigration and Customs Enforcement (I.C.E.). I was assigned to the human trafficking team, and I've been chasing Guzman for almost a year now."

Brad abruptly took a seat as he tried to assimilate what Vicky had just told them. It all seemed to make sense now, her evasiveness concerning what she had done in the Corps, her deflection of his questions regarding her job. All eyes in the room were on her now.

"Hey, I'm not here to rain on your parade," Vicky said, holding her hands out defensively, her palms facing them. "My op has nothing to do with yours. I just walked in here because I was expecting to have a little playtime with your fearless leader."

It was Jared who started it with a deep chuckle, and Jessica made it worse by giggling. It was contagious, and soon everyone in the room was roaring with laughter except Brad and Ving. Brad wore an embarrassed grin, and Ving kept a straight face. When the laughter stopped, it was Ving who spoke, though he did it without rancor.

"I understand you have a job to do, ma'am, but I'm still gonna kill the sonofabitch."

Vicky cocked her head to one side, a puzzled expression on her pretty face. "You guys don't even know, do you?" she asked.

"Know what?" Brad retorted impatiently.

"There's a black warrant out on Guzman," she said, as if her statement explained everything.

"What the hell is a black warrant?" Jared asked.

"You really don't know," Vicky said wonderingly. It was a statement, not a question.

"I know," Brad said, his face ashen. "I don't take those kinds of contracts, no matter who the sonofabitch is." He turned to his team. "The Company, the C.I.A., has a 'Wet Work' section. In short, they kill people who, for one reason or another, the government can't bring to trial. It's illegal as hell, but a number of very influential people believe it's important. I have a hard time agreeing with their methods, but I understand the necessity. I just don't do that kind of work. I'm a warrior, not a damned executioner."

Ving stared at Vicky. "You mean to say that if we off this guy the C.I.A. is willing to pay us for it?"

Vicky nodded. "Last I heard the bounty reached upwards of a million dollars."

"We're not contract killers, Ving," Brad said harshly.

"But she said the guy is trafficking in humans and by that I assume she means kids since she called him a pedophile," Jared said.

"If we have to take him out to get Delroy back I'm not going to lose any sleep over it," Brad retorted, "but we won't be taking money for it. If I have to repeat myself, we're not contract killers."

"I'm not either," Vicky said, "but I would give my eye teeth to catch the guy with evidence that might stand up in court so I could get a conviction. The government won't fry him, but I can get him put away for life without parole for kidnapping."

"There isn't a stiffer penalty for human trafficking?" Jessica asked.

"Uh-uh," Vicky said. "The human trafficking laws are all but unenforceable in a lot of countries, especially in the Southern Cone. The kidnapping statutes are much clearer, and the State

Department pushes hard for extradition in kidnapping cases."

"What if they didn't have to get him extradited?" Brad asked, a new light in his eyes. "What if he showed up in, say, Dallas or Fort Worth?"

"Then I could nail his ass," Vicky said. "I've already got enough to make a case in a U.S. court." She cocked her head to one side again inquisitively. "Are you thinking what I think you're thinking?"

"I'm thinking that if we can find Delroy and he's still alive and well we should bring an extra guest along for the ride when we return to the States," Brad said. His mission face was back in place, and he met Vicky's luminous green eyes with a steady gaze. "Would you mind giving us just a minute?" he asked. "Please?"

Decision

"I'm not going to beat around the bush, guys. I like the idea of bring that bastard Guzman back to the States to stand trial. I know Ving here wants to kill the guy for kidnapping Delroy, but I don't want to kill him if I don't have to, I'd much rather send him to ADMAX for life." The United States Penitentiary, Administrative Maximum Facility (ADMAX) is the Federal maximum security prison for male inmates located in Fremont County, Colorado. It is the most secure facility in the continental U.S.

"What I want to know is whether you're willing to take Vicky on as part of the team on this mission … if she's willing to agree to our rules and wants to come along."

"We don't really know much about her other than the fact that she's easy to look at," Jared protested.

"And that she likes being looked at," Chuck added, which earned him a jab in the ribs from Jessica.

"She was a Marine," Ving said slowly. "Once a Marine, always a Marine." He looked up at Brad and nodded. "I still want to kill the sonofabitch, but if we can catch him without getting anybody hurt I'm good with it. Besides, I watched her move… I'm thinking she's got some serious skills we haven't even seen yet."

"You have no idea," Chuck murmured, which earned him another, much harder, jab in the ribs from Jessica.

"I've been wondering if we weren't going into this a little understrength anyway," Jessica said reasonably. "She was a Marine; don't they teach the same basic skills to all Marines? She was a cop in the Corps, surely she's not helpless." She looked around for some support from the others.

"You think we should invite her to come along?" Brad asked.

"I think it's a great idea," Jessica countered, "and, besides, she's been chasing this Guzman guy for a year she said. Has it occurred to you Neanderthals that she may have some highly useful information regarding this guy stuck in her head? Or were you all just thinking about how she looked in that swimsuit?" She gave Chuck another jab in the ribs.

"Hey, what did I do?"

"I knew what you were thinking, darling," Jessica said sweetly.

"She was in the Corps, and she was C.I.D.," Pete said slowly, "I say we ask her to come along."

"What do the rest of you think?" Brad asked.

The Briefing

Jessica was picked to go outside and bring Vicky back in. The two came back smiling at each other, arm in arm, a few minutes later. "I already asked if she wanted to join our merry band of ne'er do wells," Jessica said primly.

"And I said hell yes," Vicky said with a smile. She turned to Brad. "Why don't we start with you telling me what you already know and then I'll fill in the rest of what I know? That way we won't waste a lot of time with redundancy."

Brad didn't see her offer as an impingement on his authority, but he felt constrained to make sure that she understood who was in charge anyway. "You understand that if you come along as part of the team you're going to have to follow my lead, right?"

Vicky stared at him for a moment, but there was no animosity in her gaze. "I understand."

"Good."

That was all that was said, but Brad realized instinctively that a line had been crossed. There would be no more playtime until the mission was complete, if then. They were now in a strictly professional relationship. He understood that Vicky had rules of her own.

He directed her to a seat around the table and began his briefing again, starting with Delroy's mission and abduction and ending with his charter of the G-450 to transport Ving, Pete, and Jared to Cabo San Lucas.

When it was over, Vicky sat back in her chair and stared silently at the ceiling, gathering her thoughts. When she was done, she looked over at Brad. "Would you mind lending me a shirt? Somehow I don't think I should give this briefing in a bikini." She smiled at him as she asked, but it was not the flirty smile she had given him at the cantina, it was cool and professional.

Brad got up and went to his bedroom, coming back with a khaki colored guayabera shirt that would fit her like a baggy dress, covering the most interesting parts of her body except for her incredibly long and shapely legs.

"As I told you earlier, I'm an I.C.E. agent, we're part of Homeland Security now you know, and I investigate child exploitation and trafficking. Much of my work takes place in the Southern Cone." She stopped and poured herself a cup of coffee from the carafe on the table then took a sip and set the cup down.

"I guess I should start with a short explanation of just how serious this situation is and what you can expect to see when we get to Iquitos."

"I thought you said you hadn't been to Iquitos," Jared interrupted.

"I said we've had no hint of Guzman being in the area," Vicky said, "I didn't say I hadn't been there." She paused. "In fact, I've worked in Iquitos, I have friends there."

"Just to let you know what I'm doing, here are a few facts you may not be aware of. Trafficking women and children for sexual exploitation is the fastest growing and most profitable criminal enterprise worldwide, even though international law and the laws of a hundred and thirty-four countries now make trafficking a crime.

"Roughly twenty-one million adults and children are bought and sold worldwide every year for the purposes of forced labor, bonded labor, and sexual exploitation. Estimates run higher, but two million or more children are forced into the global commercial sex trade. Our figures indicate as many as six hundred thousand of them come from the U.S. alone.

"The victims typically range from eleven years of age to fourteen years of age, though we have recovered much younger and considerably older victims. Sixty percent of the trafficking survivors were taken for sexual purposes. Once upon a time, we assumed that females made up almost ninety-eight percent of the victims, but newer studies show that nearly fifty percent are young boys."

"Jesus!" Jessica breathed.

"Understand that these numbers are more than just conjecture and less than absolute fact. The truth is that there are tremendous numbers of kids who disappear every year and simply aren't reported. Runaways, unwanted children, victims of abuse… Most of them do everything they can to avoid the police."

"Why isn't this all over the news?" Pete asked, horrified.

"The information is available to the public; you can find it on the internet. Once in a while one of the news programs will mention it or do a special on it, but the fact is this is America's dirty little secret. Nobody *wants* to know about it. There are only four of us at I.C.E. who work this area full time, and the other alphabet agencies are similarly restricted. Most of the time I feel like the little Dutch boy with his finger in the dike."

"What's the Southern Cone got to do with all this?" Pete asked.

"The kids are 'collected' in the U.S. by both organized crime families and gangs, who sell them to the dealers. The easiest and quickest way to get them out of sight and mind of the U.S. authorities is to get them out of the country as quickly as possible, and that is through Mexico. There are few restrictions or inspections traveling south. From Mexico they are transported to Venezuela, Ecuador, Peru, and Brazil. Most of the kids taken to Venezuela are put on ships and transported to the child slavery markets in Europe, the Middle East, and Africa."

"How the hell can it be more profitable than the drug trade?" Ving asked. "I've seen stacks of cash that defy description after drug busts."

"Low overhead, low maintenance, and high prices," Vicky answered quickly. "The basic product costs them nothing to acquire, and they don't feed them much, so the upkeep is low. They move the kids out to the sellers fast, so there's not much to housing them."

"Yeah, but still..."

"The going price for a blonde-haired, blue-eyed child in the country of Chad is a little over half a million dollars according to the latest reports, even higher if they're particularly pretty, and spectacularly high if they are twins. The Middle Eastern markets take the cream of the trade, and their prices are much higher. When you start adding up the numbers, you can see how, after expenses, the trafficking trade is much more lucrative than the drug trade. There are fewer intercepted shipment losses and a smaller volume of transactions with larger payouts."

Vicky walked back to the head of the table. "Frankly, enforcement of existing statutes is feeble and sporadic and successful prosecution is almost nonexistent. The sad truth is that the risk of traffickers actually getting caught and punished is almost nonexistent. Drug lords get prosecuted or assassinated."

For nearly an hour she described the horrors she had seen and told them stories the survivors had related to her, particularly the ones she had heard concerning Guzman.

"Aside from finding the kids in wretched surroundings and scared to death, the hardest thing about these investigations is keeping yourself from laying waste to all the captors and handlers." Her face was a mask of controlled fury, and no one on Brad's team had any lingering doubts that she was a warrior as much as they were.

She gathered her composure once more. "Rodolfo Abimael Guzmán. Some say he's a grandson of the first leader of the Shining Path, Abimael Guzmán. Other records indicate he is more likely a distant cousin of Guzmán the elder, a one-time professor of philosophy and, incidentally, connected to the Reynoso drug cartel by marriage.

"I have tramped all over the Brazilian side of the Amazon basin trying to chase the bastard down. In conjunction with Brazilian authorities I've managed to shut down four camps where children were being held prior to being shipped overseas to the markets. We found six other camps, but somehow they'd gotten advance warning that we were coming and there was no one there when we arrived. I've gotten whiffs of Guzman's involvement there, but this is the first hard intel I've gotten that he's in Iquitos."

With Vicky's presentation over, the room fell quiet. The simmering anger of the team remained a palpable presence.

"I think Ving is right. We need to kill the sonofabitch."

Brad didn't look up to see who had muttered the words, and they were spoken so softly that he didn't recognize the voice. He was far too caught up in his own emotional turmoil to care.

Chapter 5

A & E Aviation

Eggers

Day 2, 0800 Hours Local Time

Brad returned the rental Suburban at the main terminal of Cabo San Lucas International Airport and had the attendant give him a ride back to the private terminal where the pilots were running up the engines of the G450. Vicky and Jessica were chatting together on the tarmac and the others were already aboard.

Brad ushered the two women aboard, and he noticed that Pete was cramped into the copilot's seat and wearing a headset. He wasn't surprised. Pete was a hell of a pilot and he loved to fly, and he never wasted an opportunity to con someone into letting him fly. Brad knew Pete carried copies of his certifications around in his wallet just in case he got an opportunity with someone he didn't know well.

The others had scattered around the seats in the plane, but the uniformed copilot was sitting comfortably in the first seat. He was watching Vicky and Jessica with undisguised interest as Brad boarded. Once Brad was seated the copilot reluctantly took his eyes off the two women and went to secure the entry door. Moments later, a grinning Pete began to taxi the sleek aircraft towards the runway.

Brad settled into his plush leather seat and reclined. As near as he could figure, the flight would take roughly seven hours, a little over twenty-six hundred miles. He tried to focus objectively on the information Vicky had given them in her briefing. Try as he might, his focus kept shifting back to the woman instead of the briefing. Eventually, he gave up and settled back, reminding himself that sleep itself is a weapon a warrior cannot afford to ignore.

Landing

The reverse thrusters of the jet engines made enough noise to rouse Brad from his sleep. The others were already awake and looking out the round windows by their seats ... with the notable exception of Ving. Ving continued leaning forward on the edge of his seat, a determined scowl on his face. Brad chose to say nothing. Ving had given his word he would be on his game for this mission, and this was no time to doubt him.

Brad stepped off the stairs and onto the tarmac, stretched and yawned. He glanced down at the Hamilton chronograph on his wrist and noted that it was 1500 hours Cabo San Lucas time. He had forgotten to set his watch to Cali time, which was in the same time zone as Dallas. A quick mental calculation told him it was 1700 hours in Cali, and he adjusted the timepiece accordingly.

A man in his mid-fifties with a brown horsehide leather bomber jacket was waiting for them in front of another Suburban, this one proudly displaying the logo of A & E on its door. Samuel Eggers was a man of medium build with a bald spot that left a circle of short salt and pepper hair on his head resembling a monk's tonsure. He stepped forward to give Brad a quick bear hug and then did the same to Ving.

"How are you holding up, Ving?" Eggers asked.

"I'm okay, Chief..."

Brad sort of expected Ving to say more, but Vicky and Jessica, trailed by Chuck, were walking towards them and the conversation came to a halt as Brad made the introductions. Several hangar employees came out to help with baggage and to tie the plane down. Eggers clapped Brad on the shoulder.

"We should probably get on out to the office now. I've got a lot of arrangements settled, but I need to get more information from you before I go any further." He led Brad and the others to the big three-quarter-ton SUV and shepherded them inside. When he entered the driver's side door, he began a lively monologue about how the aviation leasing industry was doing better than ever in Cali.

Ackerman

Day 2 1730 Hours Local Time, Cali, Columbia

The Suburban carried them to a compound surrounded by an eight-foot hurricane fence. An area nearly the size of two football fields enclosed three hangar-sized Quonset huts and one smaller one. Lieutenant Colonel Richard Ackerman,

U.S.M.C. (ret.) met them at the door to the smaller hut and invited them inside.

Ackerman had a thick shock of spiky, red hair and a lumberjack's body—broad-chested with burly, strong arms, narrow hips, and sturdy legs. At first glance he appeared younger than his fifty-five years, but, upon closer inspection, the lines and crinkles at the corners of his smoky-blue eyes gave him away. When Eggers introduced Ving, Ackerman's eyes narrowed and his face took on a determined look.

"It's your brother those bastards have taken?"

Ving nodded.

Ackerman ran his eyes over the whole group and then lingered for a moment over Vicky and Jessica before coming back to study the men once more, and then settled on Brad. "Sam says you two were Force Recon?"

"Yes sir, and so were Pete and Jared."

"And you two?" Ackerman turned back towards the women.

"Marine Corps, C.I.D.," Vicky said. She didn't say a word about being a special agent for I.C.E. Ackerman turned his head to Jessica, by far the youngest of the group.

Jessica bowed up, her eyes flashing fire and her jaw jutting out. "I can hold my own!"

Brad, Ving, Pete, and Jared all tried to muffle their laughter and Jessica looked surprised when they completely failed to do so. Ackerman looked perplexed.

When the laughter was under control, it was Ving who spoke out first. "Colonel, I've seen Jessica face down a stampeding herd of elephants ridden by armed pygmies in the Congo. I'd trust her with my back any time."

"And I'll testify that she can hold her own in a firefight with a buttload of white supremacists in arctic conditions," Charlie said solemnly.

Ackerman turned to Brad with a look of disbelief on his rugged face.

"All true, Colonel, and more besides. If she wasn't squared away she wouldn't be with my team. She's no slacker, and, despite her appearance, she can get mean as hell when she's crossed."

Ackerman turned back to Jessica. "My apologies, Miss Jessica. It seems that you have some admiring champions. I'm afraid I let my eyes make a judgement based on appearance rather than on substance."

Jessica gave the man a wry smile. "No apologies necessary, Colonel. Lots of people have made that mistake. Fortunately for *most* of them, it wasn't fatal." There was no holding back the laughter after her response, even Ackerman broke up.

Eggers walked over to a whiteboard and tacked up an aerial chart. He picked a pointer up off a desk, a wooden dowel with a .50 caliber cartridge case on one end and a matching bullet epoxied to the other. He took up a position reminiscent of every military instructor Brad had ever taken a class from and began to tap different spots on the chart.

"A & E Aviation has branch offices here, here, here, and here." Each "here" was punctuated with a tap of the bullet head against the chart. The last "here" was at Iquitos.

"We service active oil rigs, transport maintenance teams and engineers to pipelines, transport geological survey teams to potential drilling sites, and ferry supplies to all of the above." He crossed his arms, the pointer angled towards the ceiling. "My branch manager in Iquitos has had several run-ins with a bunch of lunatics calling themselves 'Senderistas' and claiming to be members of the Shining Path movement.

"You guys should know that, a few years back, the Peruvian government declared war on the damned communists and all but wiped them out. Our contacts at the State Department tell us there are only around three hundred and fifty members left in the whole damned country, and only eighty or so are actual fighters. We've been told that they're concentrated in the VRAEM, the valley of the Apurímac, Ene and Mantaro Rivers. No one in the local governments is willing to admit that there's a splinter group of them so far north as Iquitos.

"I don't really think the locals are corrupt, their reluctance to acknowledge the problem is due to the fact that Iquitos is one of the highest crime areas in Peru already. Tourists are advised not to travel the roads at night because of all the robberies and carjackings. Despite the crime, tourism remains the biggest source of income in Iquitos and they don't want that to dry up because of the lunatics so the locals just look the other way when it comes to the activities of the Senderistas. As far as they're concerned, if they don't acknowledge the problem, it doesn't exist."

Eggers started to pace in small circles, still talking. "The 'Senderistas', I keep calling them that for lack of a better word… The truth is they're just a bunch of drug thugs, avoid the local cops like the plague. They're focused on their cocaine business, and lately they've been involved in another operation so hush-hush that nobody will talk about it. Hell, even the Federales stopped coming around after the second set of officers was ambushed and killed."

"Kids," Ving said in a ragged voice.

"Huh?"

"Kids… They're selling kids for perverts to play with."

"Jesus Christ," Ackerman exclaimed. "That's what they've been up to?" His face looked white as a sheet.

"Yes," Vicky said, "that's what they're up to."

"Why the hell hasn't the U.S. government stepped in to do something about this?" Ackerman asked angrily.

Brad and Vicky exchanged glances, and Brad nodded his approval.

"We didn't know Guzman and the Shining Path were in Iquitos..."

"We?" Ackerman asked, "I thought you said you were a Marine."

"I was a Marine, now I'm a special agent with I.C.E. I've been working child exploitation and trafficking in the Southern Cone for the last two years. I'm officially on vacation, but I learned about Guzman by accident when I met Brad in Cabo San

Lucas. I wanted to check the story out on my own time and they were nice enough to let me come along."

It wasn't quite the truth, but it wasn't a lie either. The truth was that she knew if she came with Brad's team her hands wouldn't be tied like they would if she was here officially. Brad's offer to snatch Guzman and take him covertly to Dallas sounded just too good to pass up... She might never get an opportunity like this again, Guzman would never go to the U.S. of his own volition.

"I thought this was concerning your brother being kidnapped and held for ransom by the lunatics," Eggers said, staring at Ving.

"That's how it started," Brad said. "We didn't find out about the kids until we met Vicky."

"What a fuckin' mess!" Eggers exclaimed, throwing his hands up in the air in frustration.

"Nothing much has changed," Brad said. "We're still here to get Delroy back; we just want to take one more person back with us when we go."

"What?"

"Guzman. We're going to transport Guzman back to Dallas and Vicky's going to arrange for him to be taken into custody there."

"I'm officially in Cabo San Lucas," Vicky explained. "There's no record of me leaving the country. We're going to render Guzman unconscious, transport him to Dallas, and alert the I.C.E. office of his location with an anonymous phone call. One of the guys will stay to observe until Guzman is taken while the rest of us return to Cabo."

Eggers turned to face his partner. "I don't think Rodrigues is gonna go for this, Richard."

"He'll go for it, Sam, he's just not going to get directly involved… He can't afford to and neither can the rest of the expats."

"Who the hell is Rodrigues?" It was Pete who spoke this time.

"Albert Rodrigues. He's a retired Special Forces colonel living in Iquitos as an expatriate, kind of the spokesman for the expat community there," Ackerman said.

"Sort of hell, he's the leader," Eggers said. Ackerman gave him a warning glance. "They're going to find out sooner or later, Richard."

Ackerman sighed. "I suppose you're right." He faced the group. "Al Rodrigues is a personal friend. He's also the man who's going to supply the weapons you need for this op." He paused a moment to let that sink in.

"Al has an absolutely amazing assortment of ordnance stashed somewhere around Iquitos in a secret location. I've known the man for forty years, I'm the closest thing to a brother he has, and even I don't know where he keeps the stuff or how he gets it here." Ackerman took a breath. "I told him of your request to let your men in to select their own weapons, but he refuses."

There was grumbling from the group, but Ackerman held up his hand. "He has, however, heard of you, Brad. Apparently you have a few mutual acquaintances who speak very highly of you. Al says he will take you in personally, but you will have to consent to be blindfolded from the time you leave my compound."

Brad stared at the red-haired man. "I don't think so." He said it flat, his voice cold.

"It's either his terms or you find some other place to get your weapons, Mr. Jacobs. He said to tell you it's not negotiable."

Brad was coldly furious. Everything about this mission was contingent upon his ability to get weapons in Peru. Crossing the border with drugs posed no problems for the cartels, who kept the Federales at bay with deep pockets and threats of violence against their families and friends, but they were hell on everyone else. There was virtually no chance of getting weapons into Peru on his own.

"He also said if you had a problem with that, I should say the word 'Trafalgar' to you. Does that have some special meaning for you?"

Brad jerked as if someone had shocked him with a cattle prod. "Trafalgar" was the code name for a mission he had participated in when he was a brand-new buck sergeant. It had been a highly secret one-man penetration of an Al-Qaeda stronghold, and only one other man had been privy to the details, and that had been his commander. The commander was a man Brad had admired and respected more than any man he'd ever known except for his father ... and he was currently the commandant of the Marine Corps.

In order for this Colonel Rodrigues to know the significance of the word "Trafalgar" to him, he had to have the trust and respect of the commandant, which clearly meant to Brad that the man was trustworthy. He met Ackerman's gaze. "Okay, I'm in."

The others were taken aback by Brad's abrupt turnabout, but they all knew better than to question his judgment. Brad was a man whose character generated respect in his friends and subordinates.

"Fine, can you hold on to your charter jet for another hour or two?"

"Sure, they weren't planning on leaving until this evening. The pilots are a little tired, but Pete's certified, and he got familiarized with this particular bird on the trip down so he can spell them in the cockpit."

"I'll let Al know when you go wheels up."

"Thanks Colonel."

"One more thing, Brad…"

"Yes sir?"

"Chief Eggers is going to be free for the next few days, and we just happen to have a Blackhawk available at Francisco Secada Vignetta International Airport… We have a branch office there. Do you think you could put a hot bird and an experienced chopper jockey to good use for the next couple of days?"

Brad grinned and stuck out his hand. "Thanks Colonel, I'm grateful."

Chapter 6

Iquitos

Day 2 1816 Local Time, Iquitos, Peru

The team was silent on the ride back to the airport, except for Chief Eggers, Ving, and Brad, who chatted amiably about old times the whole way. When they parked the Suburban and walked towards the G450, Vicky turned to Jessica.

"What just happened back there?"

"I have no idea," Jessica said, "but I'm not questioning it. I think Brad's on a roll." The two women laughed and linked arms as if they were going shopping in the Galleria Mall in Dallas instead of going to the most dangerous city in Peru.

The flight took a little less than an hour, and the tension built as the craft approached Vignetta International. Brad gave specific instructions to

101

Ving and Jessica about finding a place for the team to assemble, someplace where they wouldn't attract much attention. He had finished articulating that part of his plan when Eggers made a suggestion that made more sense.

"Why don't you check into one of the tourist hotels near the airport and use one of our smaller hangars as a base of operations? Our place is at the south end of the airport, it's in a wooded area that will give you a chance to prep or rehearse in private out of sight of curious eyes ... and you'd better believe there will be eyes on you as soon as we land.

"One thing's for certain, there are no secrets from the criminal element in this little town. As soon as the word gets out you guys arrived in a private jet every lowlife in the city is going to be drawn to you like flies."

"I should have considered that before we decided to come on the jet," Brad muttered.

"I think I can fix it," Eggers said smugly.

"What have you got in mind?"

"First, we all stay on board the aircraft until I can get a limo to come out and pick us all up..."

"I thought we wanted to avoid attention..."

"I ain't done yet, Sarge, hold your horses..."

Brad nodded and held his hands out, palms up.

"When the limo pulls up, we all go get in it, laughing, talking, and joking like we are here to party. You"—he pointed his index finger at Brad—"stay on the plane and let the pilots taxi over to the charter hangar. Colonel Rodrigues is going to pick you up there anyway and take you to wherever the hell his warehouse is. I doubt that it's anywhere near Iquitos, so I figure it will take a while. You can use that fancy satellite phone of yours to call me when you get back to the airport, and I'll bring the others to you."

Brad chuckled. "You could have just saved me the trouble, Chief, and told me that before I bent Ving and Jess's ears with my instructions."

Eggers grinned. "Good training!"

The Marines on board laughed at the worn out expression that none had heard in a while, and Jessica stared at them as if they were aliens. Vicky took pity on her and explained that "Good training" was a standard response to questions about why troops were engaging in repetitive training, housekeeping or downright 'make work' chores when the leader had no reasonable answer. It was a phrase heard many times over a tour in the Corps or any other branch of military service.

When they made the approach and landing to the airport, Pete came back from the cockpit to sit with the others; Brad went to the cramped onboard lavatory and closed the door. Eggers contacted a limo service and less than fifteen minutes passed before the stretch Lincoln Town Car arrived at the aircraft apron where the jet was waiting.

The customs officers followed the limousine out to the plane; apparently they had been keeping an eye on the jet from the main terminal, which Vicky thought was more than a little curious.

The uniformed men obviously recognized Eggers and liked him, and they gave everyone's passport only cursory glances and then stamped them on the spot. Eggers invited them to join him in the airport lounge for 'refreshments', which turned out to be drinks from a very expensive bottle of Macallan scotch that the bartender took from beneath the highly polished bar. Vicky noted that there was a strip of tape across the back of the bottle marked "A & E".

Eggers saw her notice the tape and gave her an exaggerated wink before raising his glass in a toast to the two customs officers. No one in the lounge seemed to consider it strange that the customs men were drinking on duty.

The jet rolled into the charter company hangar and half a dozen men in maintenance coveralls rushed out to begin cleaning off the exterior of the Gulfstream. "We're not getting off the aircraft," the pilot told Brad. "That's why the customs guys didn't come aboard.

"Technically, we're not supposed to open the door while we're in here to get wiped down, and we'll stay aboard when we roll back outside to refuel." He smiled at Brad. "Jake didn't tell us one way or the other, so you tell me. Are we through here or are you going to extend the charter?"

"Yeah. Wait till I get out of here and then call the tower and tell them you're staying for an unspecified time. Take rooms in the closest hotel and be ready to leave at a moment's notice. I'll get hold of Ving and have him take care of the rooms and meals."

He grinned at the pilots. "Try not to drink all the booze in the bar." The two men laughed. This was not the first time they had flown for Brad, and they were aware that he knew neither of them was a drinker.

The last of the maintenance men was picking up rags off the floor when Brad opened the cockpit escape hatch and peered out. He waited until the man had gone to get the tractor driver to tow the aircraft out to the refueling station before quickly crawling out the hatch and dropping to the ground. As lightly as he could manage, he ran for the side door of the hangar, where he'd been told that Al Rodrigues should be waiting for him.

The blocky SUV was waiting where Colonel Ackerman had said it would be, beneath an exterior light that was conveniently either broken or turned off. Brad climbed into the back seat with the passenger, who spoke with a whiskey roughened voice as he extended his hand. "I hope you're Brad Jacobs. I sure as hell didn't plan on killing anybody tonight."

Brad took the proffered hand. "Well, I'm Brad Jacobs, so I guess you're being spared the trouble." He said it lightly, but the shadowy figure in the back seat didn't think his response was cute.

"The commandant said you were one of the best, and I hope he's right. I'm taking a hell of a risk doing this … not only me but the whole expat community." The figure sat up straighter and Brad managed to see his face in the dim light. It was the hawk face of a stern man, a face used to the responsibilities of command, a face that had seen war. There was no fear in the face, but there was caution.

"Tell me about the risks," Brad said.

"Put this on and I'll tell you on the way," Al Rodrigues said, handing Brad a black bag with a drawstring closure at the top. Brad reluctantly slipped the bag over his head and pulled the drawstring merely tight enough to keep the bag from coming off.

Rodrigues wasted no time in getting started. "Sam says you're one of the good guys, and the commandant agrees with him. I'll tell you right now that the only reason you're coming in here is because those two men vouched for you and said you could be trusted."

"So why am I wearing this bag over my head, sir?"

There was silence for a second before Rodrigues answered. "I've made sort of an unofficial study of brutality and atrocities since I was a kid.

"I read about how the Comanche roasted their prisoners alive, hanging them upside down over a slow fire. I read about the Japanese in World War II and what they did to the people of Nanking in 1937. I read about the Viet Cong and how they tied our troops to the ground and partially eviscerated them, leaving them staked out at night and listening to their screams at night when the jungle predators came out to feed on the open wounds. Then I saw for myself how the Somali warlords tortured their own people and what they did to our troops when they captured them.

"What I saw sickened me, I had trouble accepting what I was seeing with my own eyes… I almost got out of the Army after that." He sighed.

"I didn't expect I would ever see worse than what I saw in Mogadishu, but, unfortunately, I hadn't been to Iraq or Afghanistan yet. I saw methods of torture in those places that I can't describe in words even now. I swore the Afghans were the most merciless, sadistic bastards on the face of the earth. I can tell you now that these crazy bastards you have come here after are the worst of the lot."

"I'm sorry, Colonel, but I did some time with the Afghans myself, and I have a hard time believing there are more sadistic people than them…"

"Well, you can believe it, Sergeant. I've seen these people gut a boy and tie the end of his intestines to a pole buried in the ground and force him to walk around it until there was nothing left, or at least until they couldn't make him move any more with their cattle prods. I've seen them tear a baby from its mother's breast and feed it to a pack of wild dogs and force the mother to watch ... and I've seen worse, much worse. These men go beyond ruthless, beyond heartless."

Rodrigues' voice was ragged; he was having trouble keeping his emotions under control. "When we formed our little community of expatriates here, the place was rough, but the local cops kept the criminals on the run and the Federales were at least staying even with the drug lords. The land was cheap as hell and it was easy to stockpile weapons here ... an ideal place to set up a colony where we might live as we wanted and keep all comers at bay. We wanted to be able to live as we saw fit without interference from the outside world.

"We did fairly well for a while, before this Guzman bastard showed up with his Shining Path splinter group and everything changed. The local cops were completely intimidated, and pretty soon they simply gave up. The city went wild. Eventually, Guzman's thugs started killing off the Federales, and now they just don't come around here anymore."

Rodrigues sighed. "Finally, the bastards came after us. A bunch of the expats simply called it quits and abandoned their places. Maybe thirty of us remain, and most of the families have been sent back to the States until we can get a handle on this. We abandoned our farms and scattered out over the city."

"We're too few to get into an all-out war with Guzman, so we use the expertise we learned in the military, we pick and choose lame targets, and we do as much damage as we can when and where we can. The one thing we cannot afford is for Guzman to find our stash of ordnance."

"I can understand your position, Colonel, but we're on your side here. None of us would have told anyone the location of your weapons."

"I believe you, Sergeant, at least you wouldn't voluntarily, but I saw those two women who got off your plane. Just how many body parts could you watch those savages chop off before you told them anything they wanted to know?"

Brad's silence spoke volumes.

"The only reason I agreed to this, even after Sam and the commandant vouched for you, is because we can use all the help disrupting Guzman's organization we can get. I don't hold out a hell of a lot of hope that your man's brother is even still alive. The Senderistas tend to demand a ransom and then deliver dead bodies ... if they don't just take your money and kill you out of hand. I'm not so sure they can do that to you.

"You have a pretty impressive track record of doing a great deal of damage with a small number of personnel. I hope to be able to provide you with the proper equipment to inflict maximum casualties on these guys. If, against all odds, you manage to take out a good number of Guzman's subordinate leaders, my people stand a chance of getting back our lands and homes."

"If you can't take them on with thirty people how am I supposed to take them on with the handful I brought with me?"

"Like I said, Sergeant, you have a reputation. My expats are experienced, but their average age is sixty-one. Even ten years ago we would have chewed these thugs up and spit them out. Now we simply do the best we can. You and your men are the last, best hope we have."

Brad rode in silence for a while, his mind racing. The expatriates didn't expect any help from the Peruvian government because of corruption and outright fear. The U.S. government's hands were tied unless the Peruvian government asked for their help. If a black ops mission failed or made a splash in the news there would be hellish consequences. His team was a convenient solution, and he understood why the expats couldn't help him openly, but his understanding didn't make him any happier.

"You know, Colonel, they're not only into drugs anymore…"

"Yeah, we know. They're selling kids. Just promise me one thing, Sergeant."

"What's that, sir?"

"Fuck up as many of those bastards as you can so me and my group of geezers can finish the group off."

The Warehouse

Day 2 1949 Hours Local Time, Outside Iquitos, Peru

The SUV stopped and the driver got out. Brad was able to hear him rustling and thumping outside the heavy vehicle, and suddenly the driver got back in and drove perhaps another hundred feet. From the sound of the exhaust Brad could tell they had driven into another structure of some kind, but he still had no idea what it was or how the expats managed to keep such a large building hidden from the Shining Path.

His question was answered as soon as Rodrigues lifted the bag from his head. They were surrounded by earthen walls and the ceiling was supported by timbers, like in a mineshaft. They were underground.

Rodrigues walked over to the nearest wall and found a switch. When he flicked the switch, two long rows of fluorescent lights came on, exposing long rows of canvas-covered boxes.

"I've got just about anything you want. You make your selections and Grover here will fill your order and deliver it to the A & E hangar before daylight." Grover was apparently the name of the driver.

Brad looked at the rugged looking former Special Forces colonel. "How do you want payment for this stuff, sir? I warn you, I'll take the best you've got to offer and I'm willing to pay top dollar."

"You're welcome to whatever you find here, Sergeant, but I don't want your money."

"I don't understand, sir, how do you want me to pay for this?"

"Body count, Sergeant, an extremely large body count ... and hopefully one of them will belong to Rodolfo Abimael Guzman." Brad did not reveal his plans for Guzman; taking Guzman to the States would solve the colonel's problems with the man just as well as killing him.

The expatriate stash didn't have the CAR-4s and M-240s that Brad and his team were used to, but there were plenty of M-16s and a crate of M-60 machine guns. It was all surplus, but it was all packed for shipment in the heavy brown paper it had come from the factory with. A visual inspection told Brad that each weapon had a thick coating of Cosmoline; none of them had been used.

There was a rack of sniper rifles that looked as if they had seen very little use. Brad selected a Barrett .50 from the rack and pulled the bolt back. The chamber was spotless with no sign of rust or powder, and the firing pin showed no evidence of use at all.

The last set of crates on the first row contained handguns, and Rodrigues must have seen the disappointment on Brad's face when the first crate turned out to be M-9 Berettas. He choked back a

Scott Conrad

laugh and opened a second crate containing M-1911 .45 Colts. "Some of the geezers just wouldn't make the transition to the 9 mm." Brad grinned and took one for each member of the team; he knew the preferences of everyone except Vicky, and she had specifically requested a .45.

"Colonel, you wouldn't happen to have a suppressed .22 pistol in here anywhere, would you?" Rodrigues grinned again and reached under a tarpaulin, bringing out a presentation box containing a Sig Sauer Mosquito fitted with a suppressor.

On the second row Brad was a little awed at the assortment of toys the expats had squirreled away. From the collection he selected claymore mines, hand grenades, and six M-72 LAWs. The anti-tank rockets were wonderful for taking out the heavy and sometimes armored SUVs favored by the drug lords.

"Take these with you," Rodrigues said gruffly.

"What's this?"

"Topographical maps showing the locations our scouts have determined to be holding areas for prisoners ... and children. We've had our eyes on Guzman for quite a while."

Grover wrote down his ammunition requirements and totted up the number of magazines needed then proceeded to start loading everything into a battered Ford pickup truck with a camper shell on it. Rodrigues took Brad back to the SUV and handed him the hood. "Sorry, my friend, but if they catch you, you can't tell them what you don't know." Brad put the hood on.

Chapter 7

Delroy

Very Much Alive

Day 0 minus 3, Iquitos

Delroy Ving was very much alive, though he wasn't certain how long that condition might last. The bastards who kidnapped him were not only sadistic, they were crazy as hell. The D.E.A. had sent him to the Army's language school at Monterey to learn the Quechua language before sending him undercover on a mission to northern Peru, so he understood every word his captors were saying.

He played dumb, pretending he couldn't understand them, and so far they had fallen for his ruse. Keeping his face blank while they discussed his fate had been one of the most difficult tasks of his life.

His training as a special agent for the Justice Department's Drug Enforcement Administration (DEA) was developed to prepare him for situations like this. He knew the secretary of state expected him to assist his law enforcement counterparts in Peru. But right now all he could think about was getting out alive. His mission to gather tactical and strategic intelligence on the cocaine drug trafficking problem would have to wait.

The assignment had been deep cover from the start. Delroy could make no contact at all with his supervisor or other superiors. His emergency contact was one of the American Citizens Services representatives in Iquitos, or warden, operating from the Dawn on the Amazon corner of Boulevard Malecon Maldonado. The one time he needed them he had been unable to reach either of the wardens.

Delroy arrived in Iquitos a year earlier after the State Department received an unofficial request from the Peruvian government, passed through the U.S. Ambassador to Peru in Lima. They requested assistance in clamping down on the cocaine trafficking connection between Peru, Columbia, and Brazil, specifically the Amazon Basin.

Delroy had felt slighted because he was being shunted down to what he considered the low end of the investigation, the farmers who planted and harvested the coca. The exciting part of the investigation would be at the other end of the supply chain where the money was. Miami. New Orleans. Atlanta. Places with decent restaurants and a glamorous nightlife instead of a third world hellhole surrounded by swamps and jungle, populated by critters who would either eat you, poison you or simply scare the hell out of you.

It was true that Iquitos itself remained Peru's sixth biggest city with a population of nearly half a million people, the largest city in the world unreachable by road. It was also true that there existed nightlife of sorts, but it didn't compare to anyplace else on Earth. The insects were the worst, invading even the modern places with air conditioning.

The first impression Delroy had of the city was that it seemed to be crumbling around him. There were huge areas of dilapidated mansions once owned by the rubber barons of the 1920s that had once been impressive, and there appeared still some magnificent architecture on display in the heart of the city.

In order to blend in as much as possible, Delroy found a place to rent in Belen, a section of town that looked unbelievably poor and rife with crime. The whole ambiance of the place put him in mind of Southeast Asia, even down to the tuk tuks (motocarros), the rickshas made from modified motorcycles that people used more than the rusty excuses for taxis, and the open air market in Belen where one could buy contraband openly.

He was shocked to see flesh and furs from protected animals on sale in the street stalls and also surprised to observe coca leaf and marijuana sold openly as well. The policia spent very little time in Belen, and Delroy suspected that the only ones who actually did were there to collect protection money from the street vendors and the gang leaders.

He had been startled to see signs painted on the brick walls in Belen saying, "No Al Turismo Sexual Infantil" (No Child Sex Tourism). After asking his landlady about the signs she informed him that for many years Iquitos openly engaged in the trade and that only recently had there been a crackdown on it. She then introduced him to her eleven-year-old granddaughter and hinted that the child was available if he was so inclined.

Delroy politely declined, hinting that he might be interested at a later time even though he had been sickened by the old woman's offer. To his dismay, the old woman then produced a 'grandson' and made the same offer. He suspected that neither child was related to his landlady. It took every iota of his self-control to remain calm, but he managed.

As his investigation took him deeper into the Iquitos underworld he began to hear more and more concerning the child sex trade and how it had all but replaced coca harvesting in the countryside as a source of income. There existed rumors of an organized group that provided children for prostitution rings that were also involved in the production and distribution of cocaine, but no one would give him specifics—they were afraid to.

Soon he got a reputation as a man who asked too many questions and the Iquiteños began to avoid him. Frustrated, he had returned to his apartment late one afternoon, certain he was being followed.

Surprise

Day 0 minus 2

He stopped downstairs and asked his landlady to send someone for a bottle of tequila and some fajitas from a vendor in the bazaar he trusted. Exhausted from his day's labors, Delroy climbed the rickety stairs to his surprisingly nice apartment and stripped down before stepping into the clay tile shower. The water was tepid, but after the heat of the day it felt marvelous.

Delroy had almost forgotten sending for food, and when the knock came at his door he answered still wearing the cotton towel tied around his waist. There stood the landlady's granddaughter, holding a greasy paper bag and a bottle with no label. Instead of taking the items from her, he fled to his bedroom and hurriedly slipped into a tee shirt and a pair of khaki cargo shorts. When he turned around to go back out to the living room, the girl appeared standing there in his bedroom, holding out the bag and bottle with a huge grin on her face.

"Why did you get dressed?"

His shock must have shown on his face. "You speak English?"

"Of course, silly," she said, setting the bottle and bag down on the bed and coming towards him. "You know you didn't have to," she said, her hands reaching towards the belt on his shorts. "I don't think you have anything there I haven't seen before."

Delroy frantically pushed her hands away from his belt. The kid was not behaving like any eleven-year-old he'd ever met. She was acting like a damned hooker. His mind flashed back to the landlady's introduction on his first day in the apartment and he realized that's exactly what this girl was. He decided a tough and uncaring front remained his best defense.

"I'm not paying for this; all I asked for was food, kid."

She pouted, and as if it were an accident, her too-large tee shirt slipped down over one shoulder, leaving it bare. "I didn't come up here for money. I came up here because you're nicer than the men she sells me to." She leaned forward and sniffed at his tee shirt. "And you're clean."

Delroy's mind kept reeling. This whole conversation seemed surreal, and he fought for control. "How is it you speak English?" he asked, snatching up the bag of fajitas and the bottle of chuchuhuasi from the bed before herding her towards the living room. Being in the bedroom with this little temptress was distinctly uncomfortable.

"I've always spoken English," she said matter of factly. "When I lived at home, we spoke English and Spanish. When I got here, I had to learn Quechua so they wouldn't beat me. Once I learned they stopped."

His mind became suddenly filled with questions. "Where is home?"

She looked at him as if he was crazy. "Iquitos is home now, but before the nasty man took me away I lived in Fort Worth."

Her answer prompted more questions from him. Delroy learned that her name was Liana Taylor and that her mother was Mexican and her father was an American truck driver, though her memories of them seemed faint now. She had been taken from her mother while they were shopping in a mall, and a fellow she called "the nasty man" had come up to her and told her that her mother had gone to the hospital and that he was to take her there.

Liana cooperated, and as soon as they reached his vehicle in the parking lot, the nasty man put a handkerchief over her mouth and nose. She blacked out, and when she woke up she was in someplace dark, along with several other boys and girls her age. The nasty man calmed them down and fed them, telling them he would explain later but that they couldn't go see their parents just yet.

He fed them and then herded them all into a communal shower together and made them strip down and wash with bars of plain white soap. They had all been reluctant to undress in front of each other, and in front of him, but he had been insistent. The nasty man watched them shower, especially Liana.

After they were done the nasty man toweled her off himself and helped her dress in a cheap white dress of rough cotton cloth. The other girls received identical dresses, and the boys got pants and shirts of the same material. None of them had been given shoes.

The nasty man took them to an airfield where they were shepherded onto what sounded to Delroy like an old DC-3. They were told it was just a sightseeing tour and that they would soon be returned to their families. A friendly lady with a nice smile gave them cookies and milk and that was all Liana remembered until she woke up in a battered school bus that was rattling through a gate in a high fence deep in the jungle.

Their conversation was interrupted by the landlady's knock on the front door.

"You have changed your mind about my granddaughter?" The old woman's avarice looked visible in her wrinkled face.

Delroy didn't think twice. He couldn't have given a shit what the people around Belen thought. "How much?" he asked roughly.

"How long do you want to keep her?" the old woman asked craftily. She quoted him an hourly, nightly, and a weekly rate.

"How much by the month?" he asked, barely able to contain his wrath.

The old woman thought for a moment, considering making him an offer to buy the child and rejecting the idea. She gave him a price that she thought seemed scandalous—almost half what she had paid for Liana. She looked shocked when Delroy took a wad of cash from his pocket and peeled off a number of bills without haggling about the price. Delroy shut the door behind her, and then he heard the landlady cackling loudly as she walked downstairs to her own apartment.

When he turned back, Liana flew into his arms, squealing with excitement, and then wrapping her thin legs around his waist.

"Whoa! Wait a minute, Liana," he said, lifting her up and setting her back down on the floor. She immediately began to lift her tee shirt over her head but he stopped her.

"What the hell are you doing, kid?"

Her face clouded. "Don't you want me?"

"Listen to me, Liana. You're through with that life. You don't have to do stuff like that anymore, do you hear me?" His rage was coming through and she backed away from him, scared. It took him half an hour to explain that he wasn't angry with her and another hour to make clear why adults and kids shouldn't have sex ... and he still wasn't sure she understood.

He got out of the awkward discussion by changing the subject. During the new conversation, he learned about Rodolfo Abimael Guzman and the Shining Path splinter group in Iquitos, though not the specific names. That would take more investigation to uncover, but it was a start.

After their talk, he walked Liana down to the American Citizens Services Representatives office next to the Dawn on the Amazon restaurant. He got some hostile stares from tourists who obviously questioned his intentions toward the beautiful Liana, who cleaned up amazingly well after she used enough of Delroy's shampoo and bath soap to clean all of Belen. But the citizens of Iquitos paid him no attention at all.

He pointed the office out to her and made sure she understood that if she ever had reason to believe he was in trouble she should come here and stay until she spoke with one of the wardens. Given the amount of time the office looked to be closed, her chances of getting any help from them appeared pretty slim, but it seemed the only advice he could give her that might help. He remained under deep cover, and there would be no other available help for her.

Delroy knew damned well that there were other D.E.A. agents in Iquitos, but he had no idea who they were—and he knew that they damned well wouldn't lift a finger to help Liana.

C & C (Children And Cocaine)

Day 0 minus 1

Delroy's mission had expanded. According to what Liana told him, the people the "nasty man" delivered her to lived in a barbed wire compound somewhere north of Iquitos and that the compound was across one river. When the men brought her to the landlady, Mrs. Perez, she had been brought in a vehicle she described in a way that convinced Delroy it must be an old Willys jeep.

The jeep was loaded onto a ferry and crossed a river narrower than the Amazon, which left Delroy with two choices, the Rio Nanay and the Rio Momon. There had been one more ferry, a much smaller one, which crossed over Rio Itaya to Belen, but Liana had shown him that one.

Liana's descriptions sounded remarkably detailed for someone so young, but Delroy found her to be an unusually intelligent child. Armed with her descriptions, he would recognize the ferry when he saw it. He did not want to hire a motocarro, the drivers were generally talkative fellows anyway, and they loved to gossip about their fares.

Another conversation with Mrs. Perez, who seemed to have a finger in many different pies in Belen, netted him a battered 250cc off-road motorcycle. The bike looked ridiculous carrying his 190 pound frame, but it maintained enough power to move him around, and the gas mileage was tremendous.

Delroy searched the area towards the Rio Momon first, considering the fact that there appeared very little traffic in that direction and absolutely nothing showing as far as buildings north of the river... It would be the perfect spot for a secret compound and a great place to conduct business out of sight of prying eyes.

Two days of intense searching earned him nothing but an empty fuel tank and an aching butt. He found two ferries, neither of which came even close to Liana's description. On the third day, he refueled the bike and rode up to the big ferry across the Rio Nanay. When he arrived, he knew he had discovered the ferry Liana described.

The sleepy looking attendant at the ferry stop on the south side of the river told him that the ferry only made two crossings each day, once in the early morning and once in the evening, though he couldn't give him an exact time. When Delroy pressed him for a more accurate time, the attendant finally opened his eyes fully and gave Delroy a hostile stare. "When she is full señor, she leaves whichever side she is on." It was as much information as he was able to get.

Liana's peals of childish laughter rang out when he told her what he found out.

"Silly man. How many people in Belen have you seen wearing a watch?"

Delroy had known, after the loss of an expensive Seiko Chronograph and three cheap Timex watches, that to wear a wristwatch in Belen was like painting a sign on his back in Quechua that said, "I'm stupid, rob me." The fact that the ferry only made the trip north in the evening caused another problem for him and he said so, which earned him an exasperated look from Liana.

"If you want to go across the river at a certain time, you should hire a peque peque." A peque peque was a small boat that carried tourists and well-to-do citizens of Iquitos from one spot to another along the many waterways through and around the city. Delroy felt foolish for not having thought about them, for he used them many times in the year he'd been in Iquitos.

He had been thinking of the motorcycle when he'd fixed on the ferry, but it wasn't very heavy. It could be carried on one of the peque peques operated by one of the less reputable looking rogues on the river. For the right money, those guys would ferry the devil himself across the river and it didn't take much American cash to get their blood racing. A U.S. five dollar bill was enough to hire a hit man in the right part of Belen, and the riverfront was a damned dangerous place.

River Crossing

Day 0

He got up before first light and rode to the Rio Nanay in the dark. It looked near daylight when he found a peque peque willing to ferry both him and the bike across the river. The added weight of the bike nearly swamped the shabby little boat, when Delroy looked there seemed only about two inches of freeboard, and he knew that it would only take a small wake behind another peque peque to sink them. It felt like he held his breath all the way across the river.

After what felt like an eternity, the little boat nosed up to a rickety wooden dock and Delroy and the operator struggled with the motorcycle, eventually getting it up on the dock. When the boat sped on its way downstream to seek another passenger for the return trip, Delroy trundled the bike down the dock to dry land. The bike didn't want to start, so Delroy finally push-started it and rode towards the dirt road that passed for a highway.

He passed houses and businesses on both sides of the dirt road until it petered out. With the bike idling between his legs, he scoured the surrounding jungle, seeing absolutely no sign of a road or a trail going out into the jungle. Discouraged, he turned the bike around and rode back to the last of the dwellings on the road.

He spotted a Quechua woman of indeterminate age hanging laundry in her back yard. He parked the bike and strode towards her, but he halted when he heard a low growl. The mutt came out from beneath the wobbly structure that passed for a porch on the shabby house, its ears pinned back and its teeth bared.

The woman called out sharply to the dog, who frankly didn't appear that eager to obey her, and then turned back to Delroy, an inquisitive look in her eyes. She didn't seem to be afraid of him, but she looked wary.

Delroy told her in his slow Quechua what he was looking for, a road into the interior. The woman's eyes hooded, as if to dismiss him without saying a word. When she started to turn her back to him, he pulled the wad of U.S. dollars out of his pocket and waved them at her. Her eyes bugged out when he held out a twenty, but she showed no intention of moving towards it.

"They will kill me," she whispered.

Delroy offered more, and she looked tempted, but still she shook her head no. With no hesitation he peeled off five one hundred dollar bills, the woman had probably not seen so much money at one time in her life. Her reluctance melted away. With five hundred American dollars she could move back to her family home high in the Andes, away from the drugs and crime of Iquitos.

She closed with Delroy and whispered directions to the track leading out into the jungle, where the bad men were. She didn't know what they did out there, and she didn't want to.

Delroy followed the dirt road back perhaps a quarter of a mile before he noticed the turnoff. It looked barely more than a goat trail, but the distinct tire pattern of a jeep appeared obvious once the hard pack was behind him. He crossed two muddy streams on the bike before he came to one that he couldn't ride across.

Walking upstream and downstream a ways, he found a spot that looked as if he could make it across. He then went back to collect the bike, which he trundled down to the crossing and concealed in a pile of brush.

He walked waist deep into the muddy brown water before he remembered the piranha and the unbelievable anaconda that were native to these waters, not to mention the poisonous snakes and the caimans. With a sick feeling in the pit of his stomach, he hurried across the expanse of the stream and lay panting on the ground ... until the ants began to bite at him.

Fighting the urge to scream, Delroy jumped up and shucked off his clothes, shaking them violently to get the damned carpenter ants out. They were all around him, and eventually he raced towards the path, his clothes in his hands.

Hurriedly, he slipped on his clothes and trudged down the path towards what he hoped would be the compound where Liana had come from. He almost made it.

Chapter 8

A Subtle Change

Ving

Day 2 2140 Hours, Iquitos, Peru

Brad had called from his sat phone as soon as the colonel was satisfied they were far enough away from the warehouse that he wouldn't be able to find his way back.

"I know you're eager to get after your brother, Ving, but there's no way we can get the Cosmoline off these weapons and get organized to move out tonight. We can't do Delroy any good if we get ourselves killed trying to reach him tonight and the colonel gave me some pretty valuable Intel about where he might be that you and I need to look at and evaluate. Pass the word around and have everyone grab a little shut-eye because I'm gonna give a wake-up call at zero dark thirty."

"Where the hell are we gonna keep the ordnance?" Ving asked irritably. He knew Brad was right, but the thought of his baby brother in the hands of Guzman and his thugs one more night was driving him crazy.

"Already taken care of, brother, chill out." Brad turned to Rodrigues. "How long till we get to the hotel?"

"Ten minutes max," the Colonel responded.

"Ving, I'll be there in ten mikes or less." There was silence on the other end of the connection.

"Ving?"

"Yeah, I got it, Brad... Zero dark thirty wake-up call and you'll be here in ten." Ving broke off the connection, but Brad was concerned. He needn't have been. Ving was surrounded by the team, including Vicky.

Vicky had never seen a team so tight, and she was really astounded that their presence kept Ving so calm when he was clearly terrified for his brother. It was her considered opinion that Delroy Ving was already dead. Guzman's Senderistas were known for their treachery and their ruthlessness.

She couldn't begin to count the number of ransom demands the group had made all over the Southern Cone, and she had yet to hear of one where the victim had been returned to their loved ones. Surely they must have returned *some* safely, else no one would pay the ransom. Still, she had never known one of Guzman's victims to survive, but she wasn't about to tell Ving that. He was already on a hair trigger and she didn't want to set him off.

The only member of the team who remained physically close enough to Ving to touch him was

Jessica, and she had her arm across his broad back, her head resting on his shoulder as his arm curled around her shoulders. "We're going to get him back, Ving," she whispered.

Charlie sat towards the outer edge of the room, and Vicky knew how he was feeling. He was the FNG, the fucking new guy, and while he had become close to the team during the outrageous Alaska mission that Brad had related to her on the flight down from Cabo, he wasn't fully assimilated yet. Even his obvious attachment to Jessica, which was equally obviously returned, didn't give him total acceptance.

Vicky had been fighting the surprising intensity of her feelings for Brad. She never felt about anyone the way she felt about him, and it had swamped her. A consummate professional, she forced the feelings back, at least until the team had accomplished their mission...or recovered

Delroy's body, which she thought to be a far more realistic outcome.

She wanted very much to take Guzman back to Dallas, but in her secret heart she admitted that she'd be just as happy if one of the team capped the asshole. Frankly, given the opportunity, she wasn't certain she wouldn't cap him herself.

Mixed with sympathy for Ving's brother and his predicament lay a strong and growing anger amongst the team. Vicky's information regarding Guzman's involvement in child abduction for the purpose of selling them into slavery had first horrified and then incensed the members of this close-knit team. The anger was smoldering, and even the most passive amongst them, Jessica, was feeling the desire to inflict death and destruction all over the Shining Path.

As the members of the group moved off to their separate rooms, Vicky wondered if someone was going to stay with Ving. She caught Pete's eye, and the big man nodded to let her know he would stay until Brad arrived. Fighting down her urge to stay and see Brad when he got back, Vicky went to her room and the big, empty bed it contained. Sleep wouldn't come to her.

Brad

Day 3 0400 Hours Local, Iquitos, Peru

Brad spread the maps out on the bed, and he and Ving pored over them for at least an hour. The locations of the Shining Path camps appeared spread along the border between Peru and Brazil, two in Peru and one across the river in Brazil.

"I would have thought they'd have a location much closer to Iquitos," Ving said as he studied the maps.

"That's one of the questions I have for Rodrigues when we get back out to A & E," Brad muttered.

"It's bad enough I want this bastard for taking my brother, Brad, but now that I realize what he's doing to kids I really want to bust a cap in his ass."

"I know, Ving, but we have to approach this as we would any other mission. We're professionals, and I don't want anybody going off half-assed and getting themselves, and possibly someone else on the team, killed. If you can't keep your demons under control, brother, I need you to tell me now."

Ving glared up at the closest friend he had in the world, a man he'd fought with across several continents now. "I can't believe you'd doubt me after all these years."

"We've never been trying to save your baby brother before, Ving. This is different, it's family."

"Jess is family too," Ving retorted. "You didn't bench yourself for that one."

Brad's eyebrows furrowed. He clapped Ving on the shoulder. "You're right, brother. I'm sorry I doubted you." The two men sat silent for a moment before Brad stood up, stretched, and yawned.

"Come on, we've got some weapons to clean … and remind me to test fire them this time before we get in contact with the bad guys."

The two of them picked up the small duffle bag Ving had brought in with him and left the room, waking everyone by knocking softly on their doors so as not to disturb the other guests. Brad deliberately let Ving knock on the doors of Jessica and Charlie. He didn't want to know if they had shared a bed. It was a foolish and unrealistic expectation that they should stay apart, especially considering the feelings he was having for Vicky. He put it out of his mind and went down to the concierge to get a couple of thermoses of coffee.

A & E Small Hangar

Day 3 0511 Hours Francisco Secada Vignetta International Airport

They left the hotel through the service entrance, hidden within the laundry van beneath a bundle of sheets and pillowcases so they wouldn't be spotted by unwelcome eyes. They shared the plastic cups of steaming black coffee, which was incredibly tasty and aromatic.

"Guess Juan Valdez saves the richest coffee beans for hotels in Peru," Jessica quipped, poking fun at a coffee commercial that had been popular in the U.S. when she was a child.

Even Ving managed a weak smile at her joke.

"It's the richest kind, Judy!" Jared intoned, continuing the parody.

Not to be outdone, Pete added solemnly, raising his cup as high as the sheets would allow. "It's mountain grown!"

Vicky's laughter washed over them all, somehow comforting. "You guys are freaking lunatics, did you know that?"

Tension seemed to melt out of them after the exchange, replaced with a different kind of tension, a healthier kind. The kind a professional trooper gets when amping up for a mission.

The laundry van drove into the small hangar and Eggers, who had been silent all night, jumped out and tugged the heavy canvas curtains down over the entrance. The edges overlapped by about three feet, which effectively shut in the light from the overheads, which flicked into life when the curtains were all the way closed.

"I see you kids are running a little late," Rodrigues said from his place near the light switches. He was wearing the same clothes he'd had on when he'd let Brad off at the hotel. Apparently, he hadn't been to sleep yet either.

"Somebody way back in boot camp told me that sleep was a weapon, sir," Brad said.

"You should have listened to him," Rodrigues said. It was clear to him that Brad had not slept, nor had Ving. "As much as it pains me to admit it, even the Corps manages to come up with astute observations on occasion." It was typical patter, commonplace whenever Marines and soldiers interacted.

"I decided to make things a little easier on you jarheads," Rodrigues said, pointing to a line of half barrels on stands lined up against the sides of the hangar. The half barrels were filled with solvent, and the weapons had been stripped and placed in solvent to soak. There sat four parts washers at the end of the line of half barrels, and they would make cleaning the rest of the Cosmoline from the weapons a breeze.

Ving grinned widely. "As much as I hate to admit it, Colonel, sometimes even Green Beanies come up with some pretty decent ideas themselves." Green Beanie was a reference to the distinctive headgear of the U.S. Army Special Forces. Coming from another warrior, it was an expression of respect.

"You'll find cleaning rods, chamber and bore brushes, and an assortment of cleaning brushes on the table across from the parts washers. Rags are in the boxes on the floor."

In minutes every member of the team was busily scrubbing Cosmoline from their weapons.

After half an hour Jessica gave a snort of disgust and threw the brush she was using into the half barrel of solvent. "I don't think they ever intended this stuff to come off!"

The laughter her comment generated sounded too loud, almost forced. Brad exchanged glances with Ving. The tension was palpable. Brad realized that a certain amount of tension was inevitable before combat, but this appeared excessive and he needed to contain it before it got out of hand.

"Listen up everybody, drop what you're doing and gather round." The team gathered around Brad. "We've been on enough ops together that I can tell when something is wrong. Today, something is wrong and I need to know what it is right now." His eyes met those of each member in turn. Jessica's were the only ones that revealed anything.

"I'll start with you, Jess," he said in a low voice. He had known her since she was a very small child, and he could read her like a book. "Come on, out with it…"

Jessica looked down at the dusty floor, twisting the toe of her boot in a circular pattern. When she finally looked up, Brad saw something he didn't ever remember having seen in her eyes before.

"This mission was already personal," Jessica said quietly, "because Delroy is family." She glanced up at Ving and then dropped her head again. The toe of her boot smashed down on the floor, and she twisted it viciously.

"After what Vicky told us all I can think of is that I want to kill this guy." She threw her head back. "I've read the phrase 'laid waste' in so many books and novels, and suddenly it makes sense to me. I want to find these guys and lay waste to anything they hold dear. I hate them, Brad, and I'm a little afraid of what I might do when I've got them in my sights."

Brad shifted his gaze to Jared, the next youngest member of the team. "Yeah," he said, "What she said, Brad..."

Pete didn't wait for Brad to look at him. "I'm glad she had the guts to say what we're all thinking, Brad."

Ving just stared at him. Brad didn't have to ask his closest friend what he was thinking, he knew. That left only Vicky and Eggers.

Eggers raised his hands, palms outward as if to ward off any questions. "I'm just a chopper jockey, I'm along for the ride... But if you're looking for an opinion, you guys are at war here. You're not playing cops and robbers and there are no Marquise of Queensbury rules for engaging animals like these."

Vicky remained silent, a frown on her pretty face. Brad was struck again by the profound effect this woman had on him every time he looked at her, and he wondered again for the thousandth time if letting her come along was really a good idea. Not that it mattered.

Vicky was sharp, and she was tough. After she'd learned of Rodolfo Abimael Guzman's location nothing would have stopped her from coming to Iquitos, where, Brad was forced to admit, she was safer with the team than she would have been on her own.

Finally, she spoke. "The estimates I got from I.C.E. said that Guzman has at most eighty effectives under arms. Everything Colonel Rodrigues has told you, plus what we've learned from Colonel Ackerman and Chief Eggers here, tells me that estimate was safe-sided by a considerable amount." She turned and looked at the arms Brad had brought back from Rodrigues' warehouse. "What else did you bring, Brad?"

Brad showed her the M-60 and was surprised to see that Rodrigues had added a second to the load. Similar surprises awaited him when he showed her the LAWs, the grenades, and the claymores.

"We're better off than I expected we'd be, but I'm still afraid we're going in understrength, Brad." Her frown had deepened, but the team members were paying rapt attention to what she was saying.

"We're going to have to hit these guys hard, with everything we've got, Brad, or we're going to get our ass handed to us."

Ving was the first to speak. "For what it's worth, Brad, I think she's right. We're going to have to take them by surprise, thunder and lightning."

"Yeah," Jared quipped, "we gotta dish out some of that 'shock and awe' crap!"

Before anyone else could speak, Brad broke in. "I happen to agree with all of you, but not for the reasons you might think."

He walked over to two cardboard tubes he'd left standing in the corner near to where the laundry van had stopped then brought the tubes back to the table where the boxes of rags had been. With a sweep of his arm, he pushed the boxes from the table and then opened the ends of the tubes. The rolled out topographical maps Rodrigues had given him were spread out and their corners weighted down with spare magazines.

Brad spoke quickly and concisely, explaining what Rodrigues had told him.

"It seems to me they would have a base camp nearer the city," Vicky said, rubbing the top of her head.

"They did," Brad said. "Colonel Rodrigues told me there was a camp north of the city, in this area here." His finger scribed a circle in the area north of the ferry on the Rio Nanay. "Three days ago, they packed up and left. These locations are places that the expatriates managed to follow them to. No one was able to confirm which location the children were taken to, and no one reported seeing Delroy."

"Jesus Christ," Ving moaned. The fact that no one had seen his brother was not a good sign.

"Easy brother," Brad said quietly, placing his hand against Ving's shoulder. "Just because they didn't spot him doesn't mean he wasn't there. Remember, they don't know which one the kids were sent to either. The expats are all getting older and they aren't in the shape they were in even ten years ago. Most of those guys are in their sixties. Hell, the last recon most of them can remember took place in Vietnam."

Ving didn't look convinced.

"We're going to have to split the team up, Ving. Somehow we've got to figure out a way to hit all three of these compounds at the same time."

"I think I can help with that, Brad," Vicky said. "I told you, I've worked in Iquitos before. I've got two men here I know for a fact I can count on."

Neither Brad nor Ving looked convinced, but Jessica and Charlie both brightened.

"It's the best I can do, Brad, but we have a more immediate problem... We're already light on weapons, and we've got to arm my two guys. Jared and Pete are right. We've got to hit them so hard and so fast they don't have a clue what's going on. Those M-60s are going to come in handy."

"Yeah," Brad said glumly, "but there are only two of them."

Chapter 9

A New Plan

Brad's Concerns

After the short briefing, the team returned to the cleaning of their new weapons with a good deal more enthusiasm than before. There prevailed a feeling of eagerness that had been missing before they had more or less gotten the okay to take their wrath out on Guzman and the Senderistas, though, privately, Vicky still intended to bring Guzman back to the States to stand trial.

Brad, on the other hand, was extremely concerned. Breaking the team down into three sub-teams and coordinating a three-pronged simultaneous attack in a widely spaced geographical area represented a textbook exercise in the near impossible.

It was a plan he had seen executed successfully only once, and that had been by a detachment of three fire teams taken from the same platoon of Recon Marines, men who had survived training and combat together. He had seen it fail two other times, with catastrophic results.

The crux of the problem was Vicky. She remained an unknown quantity in the equation. To her credit, she had completed the Warrant Officer core course for her specialty, which was no cakewalk, and of course she had finished boot camp. The question stood, whether she had what it would take to make an all-out assault on a defended position.

The risk remained one he did not want to saddle his team members with, but the truth was that, in order to even out the teams, each team would have to have an outsider along with them—and that was a tactical nightmare.

Brad shook it off. There seemed no other choice. The op was so blatantly in violation of international law that there was no hope of help from outside. If they were caught they would either be killed or be placed in some hellhole of a prison and left to rot.

The team would have to function effectively, and they would have to be successful. Brad suspected that Vicky still intended to take Guzman to Dallas so she could arrest him formally, but he remained determined that Delroy would come first … if he was still alive.

Delroy—that was another sore subject for him. He wouldn't admit it to Ving, but he had serious doubts whether Ving's little brother was still among the living. He had little doubt that the others felt the same as he did, with the exception of Ving. Brad felt a surge of pride in his team. Ving was a brother to them all, and they would honor that bond to the death if need be.

Even Jessica was now a member, though she'd never served in the Corps. She'd proven herself so completely as part of the team that Brad could not refuse her the right to go to Delroy's aid, even though he feared for her safety.

He sat down, grabbing another mug of coffee to help him think. There had to be a safer approach to this problem. Even if he allowed himself to fully trust Vicky, there were the two locals she planned to bring in to help for him to consider.

Brad sighed. He would have to try to come up with another plan on his own. He had no doubt Ving would be focused and deadly once they had boots on the ground and the bullets started to fly, but at the moment he was wrapped up in his concern for Delroy. Jared and Pete were fantastic fighters, but neither proved a particularly good strategist.

Charlie was wrapped up in his concern for Jessica, and, besides, Brad didn't know him well enough to trust his judgment on tactics. Vicky was gone, she and Eggers had driven into Iquitos to locate and pick up her two 'workers'. That left Colonel Rodrigues.

Downtown

Day 3 0547 Hours

Eggers drove the oldest, most battered Suburban A & E owned down the backstreets of Iquitos. "Are you sure your friends will still be here, Ms. Chance? Hell, the sun's already up."

"Oh they'll be here, Chief. They aren't party guys; they work as bouncers at the club."

Eggers snorted. "What kind of club could there be back in this slum?"

"I'm surprised you don't know about this place, Chief. Yes, it's in one of the poorer sections of Iquitos, but it is *the* place to be at night. It stays packed with chic young female tourists."

The chief snorted again. "I'm not much for dodging cutthroats and pickpockets, even on this side of the Rio Itaya." He was making reference to the fact that Belen, the most dangerous part of Iquitos, lay just across the river. Tourists were given an advisory when they arrived suggesting they not travel the local roads at night because of the robberies and carjackings, but the younger crowd paid little or no attention to the advisories. They came to party, and The Purple Iguana was a serious party place.

When Eggers parked the Suburban, he was torn between anxiety about the vehicle being stolen and Vicky going into the club alone. He resolved his concerns after she flashed the .45 Colt at him. She had field stripped and cleaned the weapon with remarkable speed, and she had rigged a temporary holster for it by tearing the bottom out of a nylon camera case. The weapon was loaded and had a round in the chamber.

This was not Vicky Chance's first rodeo. Anyone accosting her would be faced with much more than the threat of the .45, she also had a black belt in Krav Maga, a martial art little known outside its practitioners' circles. Unknown to Brad and the others, she had been the instructor for hand-to-hand combat, knife fighting, and pistol marksmanship for the 2nd Law Enforcement Battalion at Camp Lejeune for two years.

The entrance to The Purple Iguana was littered with discarded plastic drink glasses, straws, and napkins. The floor appeared covered with spilled drinks and ice, and there were still a few drunks left inside.

Vicky strode through the door unimpeded and visually searched the dimly lit bar before spotting a massive Quechua male wearing a black tee shirt and camouflage trousers. Over six feet tall with bulging muscles and shiny black hair slicked down close to his head, his name was Apo. Vicky knew him to be a good man and a trusted friend. He was also a mean sonofabitch in a fight.

"Apo!" she called out. The huge Mestizo's face split into a wide grin and he threw his arms wide, giving Vicky a big hug.

"How have you been, Miss Vicky?" he asked.

"Just fine, Apo, how about you?"

He let her back down on the floor and looked around the bar. "Making a living," he said. "Not much fun wrestling drunks."

"Have you seen Cauac lately?"

Apo grinned again. "He's depositing a rowdy drunk in the alley as we speak."

Vicky laughed. "I've got some interesting work if you're so inclined, you and Cauac both."

"Whatever it is, it's bound to be better than this crap," Apo said. "What's the gig?"

"Rodolfo Abimael Guzman."

Apo's smiling face froze. "Seriously?"

"Seriously."

"I'm in. Cauac's in too."

"Aren't you at least going to ask him?"

"I don't have to and you know it, Vicky. You know where he is?"

"We have it narrowed down to one of three places, and we're setting up an op to take him and his splinter group down hard."

"We?"

"I'll explain on the way, Apo, trust me; they're good people, some of the best."

"On the way? We're going now?"

"As soon as you collect Cauac."

"How soon is the op going down?"

"How does tonight sound?"

Apo grinned again and then ran to the back of the club. Moments later, he returned, an even larger Mestizo in tow. "Vicky!" Cauac cried, rushing to her and lifting her up in a crushing bear hug. He set her down. "Guzman?"

Vicky nodded, overwhelmed by the man's exuberance.

"What are we waiting for?"

Vicky led them out of the bar and over to the Suburban, and the two Quechua men climbed into the back seat. The big SUV settled noticeably on its springs as they sat down.

"Chief Eggers, meet Apo and Cauac. Boys, meet Chief Eggers. Be nice to him, he'll be flying our helicopter."

Eggers looked at the two men skeptically, though he was very impressed with their size and musculature. "Do either of you gentlemen have any experience with automatic weapons?"

Apo and Cauac laughed quietly.

"In answer to your question, Chief, Apo is an artist with an M-60, and Cauac is as good as anybody I've ever seen with an M-16. I've worked with them both before and I trust them implicitly. I wouldn't have brought them in otherwise," Vicky said, smiling at the two men.

"I didn't mean anything by it, I just had to ask. This yahoo we're going after is some kind of bad dude."

"We know who he is," Apo said grimly. Cauac nodded his assent.

Eggers shut his mouth and drove back to the airport.

Charlie

Day 3 0700 Hours

Brad was scribbling ideas for an assault plan onto a legal pad and then ripping the pages out, crumpling them into a ball, and tossing them into an empty fifty-five gallon drum. Each time he tossed one of the paper balls into the drum, he would get up, stare at the topographical maps, and mutter to himself before sitting back down and scribbling on a new sheet.

Jessica and Charlie had finished cleaning their own weapons, and Pete and Jared were cleaning the extra M-60. Jessica nudged Charlie with her elbow and inclined her head in Brad's direction. "See if you can help him any. He's worried and I'm not used to seeing him that way." She nudged him once more before Charlie reluctantly got up and walked over to Brad.

Brad had seemed to be having a problem with the relationship between Charlie and Jessica, so Charlie had stayed out of the man's way ever since they left Dallas.

"What are you working on?" Charlie asked conversationally.

Brad didn't even look up. "I need to come up with another way to do this," he said absently. "Too many variables in the plan I pieced together in Cabo. Guzman split his forces into three elements in three different places. We don't have enough personnel to pull off assaults in three different places at the same time."

"But Vicky said she's got two friends…"

Brad looked up, his mouth set in a straight line. "Look Charlie, I've seen you under fire, I know I can count on you in a tight spot. Vicky is awesome, but I have no idea how she's going to react in a firefight, and we're sure as hell going to be involved in at least one.

"As far as her friends go, I have no idea what kind of people she's going to bring back. D.E.A. isn't exactly known for palling around with the cream of society." He shook his head. "Besides, even if she brings back a couple of real shooters, we're a little light when it comes to ordnance. Rodrigues didn't spring this 'three different locations' business on me until after I'd chosen the weapons... I should have questioned him first."

"Is there any chance you can get more from him?"

"Hell no," Brad said disgustedly, "the expats are a bunch of has-beens with good intentions. Rodrigues has already put them at risk by helping us, he won't do it again. Besides, there's no time to arrange another meeting and go through all that rigmarole of getting out to the warehouse again." Brad ran his fingers through his buzz cut. "Dammit!"

Charlie had a sudden flash of memory, a story he'd heard from one of the C.I.A. agents he'd spent a long two years working with in Ecuador. *Shit!*

"Brad, I think I have an idea... Lend me your satellite phone!"

Puzzled, Brad handed over his satellite phone and Charlie rushed out of the hangar.

"Where did he go?" Jessica asked.

"I have no freaking idea," Brad told her. His curiosity was piqued, but he decided to leave the man be. He wasn't in any position to turn down help from any source at this point.

Charlie was in luck; his call was answered on the first ring. "Danny, I don't have time to explain right now... You're just going to have to trust me. You told me once that the C.I.A. kept weapons caches stashed in your ops areas. Did you ever work anywhere near Iquitos?"

He waited as his old friend spoke, and then he broke into Danny's conversation. "I understand all that, buddy, but there's a life at stake here, a D.E.A. special agent down here on a black op assigned by SecState. I need to raid that cache and I need to do it now. I swear I'll never tell anybody where I found out about it... Hell, I'll even make it look like a case of vandalism, but I need the location and I need it now!"

He searched his pockets frantically for a pen and paper and settled for a pencil stub and a tattered business card. "Hold on a second... Okay, fire away!" Charlie listened and wrote down the instructions as best he could on the small card. When he was finished, he thanked Danny Welton profusely and then broke the connection. Charlie stared down at the card and wondered if he'd be able to find the cache or not. The C.I.A. didn't make things very easy.

He ran back into the hangar and stopped in front of Brad. "What do we need?" he asked, slightly winded from his run.

"A battalion of infantry and some air support would be nice," Brad said sarcastically.

"Seriously, Brad, you said we needed more ordnance. What do we need? I can't come up with your infantry battalion, but I've got access to a weapons cache near here. I have no idea what's in it or exactly how big it is…"

Brad sat back and stared up at Jessica's boyfriend in disbelief. "You're kidding, right?"

Charlie raised his hand in the Boy Scout salute and gave Brad a wide grin. "Scout's honor. And it should be a pretty decent selection, the Company doesn't scrimp when it comes to toys."

"You have access to a C.I.A. weapons cache?" Brad wasn't sure this wasn't some kind of practical joke, but Charlie was not a joker.

"Let's get us a ride and go see what Santa left for us, Brad!"

The maintenance supervisor wasn't thrilled to give up the late model pickup truck that was the Company's only other vehicle since Eggers and

Vicky were already out in the Suburban. But the two strangers were guests of Chief Eggers, and the chief had been pretty serious about accommodating them. He handed over the keys reluctantly and the two men left in kind of a hurry.

The Cache

Day 3 0918 Hours

Despite Danny Welton's hurried instructions, it had taken them almost two hours to locate the cache, the entrance to which was cleverly concealed in the foul smelling men's room attached to the outside of a real dive of a bar on the riverfront. Brad stared around the twenty-four-foot-by-thirty-foot underground room in frank amazement.

The walls were of poured concrete, and there was an external power feed that supplied electricity to the lights and environmental control system. The engineering required to keep the humidity down and the water out of a sub-level room so close to the river staggered Brad's imagination. There was a desktop computer and a lamp in one corner, but it was the staggering arsenal of weaponry that surprised him most. Unlike the weapons provided by the expats, everything in the room was pristine, well cared for, and ready to use.

"Jesus!" Brad exclaimed.

"Yeah, as far as I know the Company doesn't have a real budget. They really go all out for their undercover assets." Charlie surveyed the impressive, very compact racks filled with every imaginable type of personal weapon. "This place must have cost a damned fortune." He heard Brad let out a low whistle and turned to find him holding open a large canvas suitcase, which was crammed with sealed packs of high denomination currency from different countries in the Southern Cone and including U.S. currency.

"I guess so," Brad said, zipping the bag closed. He stood up and walked to a three-level rack that held M-4s, CAR-4s, and M-27 Infantry Automatic Rifles (IAR). He took one of the M-27s out of the rack and pulled the bolt back to inspect the chamber. It was tempting, but he put the weapon back. They already had M-16s that would serve well enough, and there were only two of them available to carry out whatever they took.

He moved over to the next rack and grunted when he saw the S.A.W.s. The SAW (Squad Automatic Weapon) was a light machine gun that had supplanted the old M-60s, but fired belted 5.56 ammunition instead of the belted 7.62 rounds fired by the M-60. He looked around and found a brand-new G.I. duffel bag and slipped the M-249 into it, along with three cans of belted ammo.

"Grab another of these duffel bags," Brad barked. "Start with two more cans of this belted 5.56 and then take an assortment of the incendiary grenades... Focus on the WP (white phosphorous.)"

Charlie shuddered. He had seen the white phosphorous in action before. Once the substance was on an individual, it continued to burn as long as there was an oxygen source. Putting the flames out was damned near impossible. The thought of using one of these on another human being sickened him for a moment—until he remembered Vicky telling the team what Guzman was doing to kids.

He reached down and started to pick up the cylindrical black containers that read, "Smoke, WP, Burst Type," and stuff them into the duffel bag.

Brad had stopped to watch and noted the expression on Charlie's face. "Not to worry, Charlie, I want those so we can make sure Guzman's compounds no longer exist when we leave them. Understand?" *And if any of that nasty stuff gets on some of those bastards it's not going to bother me one bit. Anybody who would do that to a kid is going to face a fire hotter than 'Willie Pete' where he's going anyway.*

Charlie nodded that he understood.

Just as he was about to fill up the empty spaces in the duffel bag with explosives, Brad struck gold. He lifted the boxes with the advanced night vision devices used by Special Operations personnel as if they were sacred relics. He took all of them, and the batteries for them as well.

He took the squad radios sitting next to them too. The Liberator II Tactical Single-Communication Headsets were commonly used by Special Ops personnel in Afghanistan, and their range was boosted by the Modular Antenna System - Tactical (MAST™) in the carton on the floor beside the radios.

Brad finished stuffing his bag with more LAWs, and then began to pack the voids in the bag with quarter pound blocks of C-4. When the duffels were bulging, Brad slung his onto his back, slipping his arms through the shoulder straps, and then bent over to pick up a reel filled with Primacord and the MAST carton. "You pick up that box of detonators and keep them in front of you, away from the duffel bag."

Charlie gave Brad an uncertain glance, but Brad was already heading for the single entrance to the cache. Sighing inwardly, Charlie shouldered his duffel and grabbed the box of detonators. He wouldn't discover until later that the detonators were electrical and that they posed no danger to him.

Chapter 10

In Harm's Way

Guzman

Rudolfo Abimael Guzman was perturbed, to put it mildly. He had captured the American in the swamps north of Rio Momon, but not till the bastard had killed several of his best trackers. The black man put up a tremendous fight, but, in all fairness, Guzman had threatened to execute them if they did not bring the spy back alive.

It was fortunate that they were able to overcome him before he could destroy or lose his cell phone, the yellow satellite phone had been smashed against a huge jacaranda and his men brought him the shattered remains. They managed to overpower the man before he could do the same to his cell phone.

Guzman immediately turned the cell phone over to his second in command, a young man who had attended school in Iquitos and was familiar with such instruments. Guzman himself did not trust the modern electronic devices, relying instead on the "jungle telegraph", a system of relays of runners and drum messages. The young man always handled the few, very limited, messages to and from his buyers in Columbia.

Guzman insisted that any business dealings take place face-to-face in his compound in Brazil. The compound, one of three he had constructed, was located at a spot on the map marked as Engano. The main camp lay across the Rio Javari, which marked the boundary between Peru and Brazil. The other two were further downriver on the Peruvian side of the river, near spots similarly marked as Eureka and Nova Vida.

There appeared no sign of human habitation other than the clear cuts made by the lumber companies at any of the locations. Guzman was careful to keep it that way, and his compounds were well camouflaged.

When his second, a hardened twenty-year-old native of Iquitos named Jaime, had rushed into Guzman's quarters and excitedly reported that the American was in fact connected to the U.S. D.E.A., Guzman immediately ordered an evacuation to Engano. His Senderistas packed up without complaint and began the trek to Engano, following the protocols developed over a dozen or more drills. They moved out in groups of twenty, carrying what they needed on their backs.

Supplies for Guzman's comfort and their survival had been stockpiled at all three compounds over the previous year and weapons as well. Skeleton crews rotated in and out of the compounds all the time, so the jungle didn't encroach on what they had built.

The Senderistas traveled through the jungle on foot, in canoes, and by truck where the logging companies had left their boggy trails nearer the compounds. The prisoner and the children they were about to send to market went with them. Guzman and Jaime traveled on an ancient Sikorsky H-19 owned by a sympathetic follower who was not one of the Shining Path's fighters.

There were more, far more, followers than fighters, and Guzmán had been busy recruiting more very carefully and secretly over the past year. He managed to add and train another twenty men, giving him an actual complement of ninety-three fighters. All were disaffected victims of a repressive government, most were conscripts released from the Ejército Del Perú, the Peruvian Army, for one reason or another to a man they worshipped, Rodolfo Abimael Guzman.

Guzman paid lip service to the Communist message of the Shining Path movement, a movement started by his distant cousin, but in his not-so-secret heart he remained the ultimate capitalist. The men who followed him lived under Spartan conditions, and outwardly Guzman did as well. Not even Jaime knew of his secret accommodations, constructed even before he moved into the first compound outside Iquitos. Of the other three, only Engano contained a similar apartment prepared for him.

Guzman loved his privacy as much as he loved entertaining some of his younger 'guests' before selling them to intermediaries in Columbia and Brazil. He kept a girl in his Spartan apartment as well, a much older girl. She was seventeen years old and she knew how to keep her mouth shut; she also realized that if she revealed what she suspected about Guzman her bones would never be found.

Guzman lay curled up alone in the huge king-sized bed in his air conditioned subterranean apartment at the Engano compound. He did not have one of his unwilling playmates with him because he wanted to be alone, to think. The American presented a problem, but it was a problem he could deal with. He believed that, despite their refusal to negotiate, the clandestine services would pay up to retrieve their deep-cover asset.

Smiling to himself, Guzman remained deeply involved in planning the best way to expand his trafficking operations. The cocaine business was still profitable, but losing ground to his other operation, but far riskier. The U.S. government continued to put pressure on the drug lords, spending scads of money and uncounted hours of manpower harassing underlings and interdicting shipments.

They even recently imprisoned one of the kingpins from Mexico that most had thought untouchable. It had only been a matter of time before one of the drug enforcement people stumbled onto his trafficking business and that was something he must prevent at all costs. He needed to find out how much the prisoner knew before he decided whether to just kill him or to make an example out of him.

Either way, the man was not long for this earth. Leaving him alive was far too risky. Guzman's executioner was extracting everything the prisoner knew even as Guzman himself lay luxuriating in air conditioned comfort.

The Prisoner

Delroy Ving ached all over. His lips looked swollen and his tongue told him there were at least three teeth missing in his battered and bloody mouth. He quietly spat blood and spittle to the rough dirt floor, hoping the brutish and hulking Mestizo who enjoyed torturing him would not notice. He had no inclination to raise the sadistic bastard's ire.

It seemed patently obvious that the Senderistas had read the contents of his cell phone, and Delroy cursed himself for not ridding himself of it sooner, before he had been surrounded and beat down in the swamps north of Iquitos. It was scant satisfaction to him that he had taken at least two of them out before they beat him into submission. He wondered at the time why they had not already killed him, but when the mauling started, he soon figured out they wanted something from him.

Delroy scoured his brain, wondering what exactly they were looking for, and deciding what information they had already gleaned from the numbers stored in his cell phone. Fortunately, the most important numbers were stored in his head instead of in the phone's memory. Unfortunately, there were a lot of numbers in there that were of no significance to his work or his job, leaving a lot of innocents subject to the not-so-tender ministrations of Guzman's torturer.

True to his training, Delroy continued only giving up information he was already relatively certain they had gathered or guessed. What he was giving out he was giving out slowly and at a cost of considerable pain. When he wasn't praying for death, he was praying that his brother would find out what had happened and exact a price from Guzman for what he was having to endure.

He had given up any hope of rescue when he saw how far out in the Amazon Basin the Senderistas were taking him. Big brother Mason would never be able to find him, but Delroy refused to give up all hope. A tiny corner of his brain still believed that someone or something might rescue him and their efforts would be worthless if he let these bastards kill him. It was a thin strand, but Delroy clung to it. It was all he had.

The scarred Mestizo with the shaven head and the Pancho Villa mustache entered the simple grass hut where Delroy Ving sat restrained and stared at the prisoner. Uturuncu had never encountered such resistance in a prisoner. Every time he started to give up and kill the man to end the questioning, the prisoner would give up another tidbit of information and start the cycle of torture all over again.

Chapter 11

Final Planning

Breakdown

With the additional assets to employ, Brad was busily altering his plan of attack. His first alteration was the composition of three teams, one for each compound Rodrigues had given him the coordinates for. His initial impression of Apo and Cauac was very positive, they looked like warriors, and they handled the weapons Brad tossed them expertly.

Apo had taken a few minutes to examine the M-241 and turned mutely to Pete and offered to trade for the M-60 Pete held. No words were exchanged, but Pete had used the M-241 for years and he had no objections to trading for the lighter, smaller caliber M-241 at all. Apo, on the other hand, immediately relaxed and caressed the M-60. He treated it like a beloved friend, and it looked apparent to everyone that man and gun were perfectly in harmony. Apo's grin lit up the hangar as he dipped his head in thanks.

Brad broke the team down into three units, one for each assault. He took the first unit for himself, adding Vicky so he could keep an eye on her, and Charlie … more to keep his mind off protecting Jessica than for any other reason. Ving he paired with Cauac and Jessica, and Pete was paired with Apo and Jared. Eggers would fly the Blackhawk.

He couldn't shake the bad feeling he had about this mission, but he couldn't pinpoint a single cause. The idea of splitting the team up didn't sit right with him, though intellectually he knew it remained his only option. The longer Guzman kept Delroy in his possession the worse Delroy's chances of survival became.

The fact that the expats who followed the Senderistas to the compounds had seen no sign of

Delroy was a grim indicator, but Brad did not share that intel with Ving. The man seemed distraught enough over Delroy's abduction; he didn't need reminding at this point that it was highly unlikely that his baby brother was still alive. The burden of keeping his considered opinion to himself was beginning to wear on Brad Jacobs.

Insertions

Brad turned his mind to the Insertion Plan; it had to be done and it would get his mind off Ving's anguish. Brad found Chief Eggers in a corner of the hangar talking with Pete and Jared.

"Hey Chief, how about a little help with the Insertion Plan?"

Eggers turned and walked with Brad over to the table, where he leaned over and placed his closed fists atop the map spread out there. He traced his finger across the map, making an arc roughly ten miles north of the three compounds.

"How precise are your locations for these camps?"

"Pretty damned precise. Those old guys came up with an eight-digit grid coordinate for each location."

Eggers' eyebrows rose. "Old school soldiers, huh?"

"If they had a GPS they couldn't have gotten more exact." An eight-digit grid coordinate defined a spot on a one to twenty-five thousand scale map to within ten meters, roughly a thirty-foot circle.

Eggers scrutinized the map for any sign of elevations, but he also needed information about cleared areas at least forty-five meters across, large enough for the Blackhawk to sit down safely. He chewed at his lower lip as his finger traced across the map.

"You got a colored pencil, Brad?" he asked.

Brad fumbled around in his pockets and brought out a pencil with red lead on one end and blue on the other and handed it to the grizzled retired chief warrant officer. Eggers quickly circled five different spots on the topographical map and then looked up at Brad. "Can you get me the latest available aerial photographs or satellite images of these areas on your little magic box?"

Eggers was referring to Brad's laptop. Unless it had to do with avionics on his helicopters, Eggers was a technological dinosaur. He left everything about computers to Colonel Ackerman, preferring to get his hands dirty in the engine compartments of the birds they operated.

Brad's fingers flew over the keyboard, linking with Google Earth first.

"How recent are these images, Brad? You can clear cut an area in the Amazon Basin and it will cover itself up in a month, sometimes less."

Brad had run into this problem before, and he had a ready answer for the chief. "Usually, except for the most remote areas, these photos are renewed at least once every ninety days. Give me a minute and I'll check a few of my other sources." His fingers were already typing new URLs (uniform resource locator, internet addresses), accessing sites he had hacked into before.

Jessica and Charlie stood peering over his shoulders by now, watching as he sought the images Eggers needed. The problem was that, as far as Brad knew, this remote part of the Amazon had no military satellites scrutinizing it. The communications satellites were of no use to him because they didn't carry cameras. Brad was making exasperated sounds as he checked one source after another with no success.

He looked over his shoulder at Charlie. "No chance you know of any super spook agency satellite platforms scoping out this area is there?"

Charlie shrugged helplessly. The region was of no strategic value at all, and even the C.I.A. couldn't afford to have eyes everywhere.

It was Jessica who finally provided the solution to the problem. "When I came down here looking for Incan gold with Professor Sorenson, he used real-time satellite photos from a geosynchronous satellite that the major logging companies chipped in and launched a few years ago."

Brad stared at his cousin, flabbergasted. "Logging companies? With their own satellite?"

Jessica laughed. "You really should get out more, Brad. Logging enterprises in the Amazon Basin, especially the unlicensed ones, are the new robber barons of the twenty-first century. They make huge profits from harvesting first growth hardwoods that can't be found anywhere on Earth except right here.

"It's not like it was when you were a kid either… You can get a satellite launched for a few hundred thousand dollars these days. My gosh, even the Space Shuttle used to launch them for private industry for a fee. The satellites themselves are mere child's play because of all the technical advances in electronics and cameras in the last twenty years. A half million dollars, spread between four or five competing logging corporations is chicken feed."

She bent forward, brushing Brad's hands away from the keyboard, and quickly typed in a search for one of the local logging companies. From their website she accessed dated aerial photographs, selecting the territory southeast of Iquitos. She found the five locations Eggers had circled scattered over two separate photo images in a matter of minutes.

"Jesus Christ!" Eggers exclaimed.

Scott Conrad

"They don't even bother to hide them," Jessica said, pleased with Eggers' reaction. "This is available to the public."

"Jesus Christ!" Eggers repeated, bending closer to get a better look. "Is there any way we can print this out so I can take a closer look?"

Jessica laughed. "You really are a dinosaur, Chief!" She moved the cursor to the top right of the monitor and clicked on an icon then moved the cursor down a drop-down menu to the word 'zoom' and started to enlarge the photos.

"Jesus Christ!" This time it was Brad exclaiming as a clearing perhaps two hundred and fifty meters wide and miles long began to grow before his eyes. As far as they could see, tree stumps were cut off level with the ground. Here and there clumps of vegetation and debris lay stacked up.

It was apparent that the clumps had been set afire and left to burn. Most had burned and left a pile of

207

ashes, but many remained, their fires burned out. No one stuck around to monitor them. It was a sad and sickening sight, total devastation of a landscape that had been left untouched by man for millennia.

They found three such areas within twenty miles of the Nova Vida compound, the center of the three Shining Path compounds.

"Holy shit, Jessica, can you get the photos of the area where the compounds themselves are?" Brad was excited. A great deal of his trepidation regarding this mission had been due to his total lack of intelligence about the compounds themselves. The photos of the clear cut areas had been dated only three days before.

Jessica said nothing, she just clicked on an adjacent image and the four of them were looking at a twenty-mile section of the Rio Javari. Some spots along it appeared obscured by cloud cover, but two of the compound locations had no obstructions. As

Jessica enlarged the Engano location, the four of them let out sighs of disappointment.

The section where the grid coordinates pinpointed had been deliberately blurred. Guzman had some kind of leverage over the logging companies, enough to get the images altered. The other unobscured compound, Eureka, looked similarly blurred.

Frustrated but not daunted, Eggers finally located areas within walking range but out of earshot of the compounds where he could at least hover a few feet off the ground and release his passengers.

Rehearsals

Brad despised going into any tactical situation with so little information, much less with personnel he hadn't fought with before. He was winging it, he knew it, and he hated it. His willingness to forge ahead under the impossible circumstances was a measure of the respect and affection he had for Mason Ving and because of the awful predicament of the innocent children Guzman and his thugs intended to sell into slavery.

He tried not to think about the horrors those kids had no doubt already been subjected to because it made his blood boil to do so, and he needed a clear head for this op. He wouldn't be able to do Delroy or the children any good if he allowed his team or himself to be killed in a failed attempt.

Still apprehensive, Brad scratched out as detailed an operations order as he could on the remaining pages of the yellow pad. When he was finished, he called Ving over and had him review the order. While Ving was reading, Brad called Jared over and assigned him the task of checking to see that everyone possessed the proper equipment. "What about test firing the weapons, Brad?" Jared asked.

"Shit!"

"I could crank up a couple of the choppers," Eggers volunteered. "Nobody will find that out of the ordinary, and unless one of your '60 gunners gets carried away, nobody's going to hear a few gunshots over the sound of two Chinooks running full bore."

The Chinook, the civilian version of the venerable CH-47, was powered by two Lycoming 4,733 horsepower engines. The unmuffled exhaust of four such engines would effectively drown out the noise from small arms fire. Eggers looked up sharply as if someone had just hit him with a brick.

"You still plan on trying to take these guys out at night, Sarge?"

Startled, Brad returned Eggers' stare. "Sure, I don't think I've ever conducted a daytime assault if I had a choice. One of the basic tenets of ground combat is to control the time and location of your battles."

"Yeah," said Eggers, "but these guys aren't accustomed to the sound of choppers flying at night, and they ain't used to these little ones either. The loggers use the Chinooks to move equipment and the more valuable logs and they do it in the daytime. On top of that, Sarge, how you gonna get those kids out of the jungle when you blow away those rat-bastards holding 'em?"

Brad's jaw dropped, and everyone in the hangar turned to gape at Chief Eggers, who had just thrown a monkey wrench into all Brad's plans. The reason they stared was that the man was right, and it hadn't occurred to a single one of the combat hardened veterans of the team. Eggers had just given them back the element of surprise.

Exhilaration flashed through every one of them as Eggers' observations registered on their brains. Brad saw his mistake as soon as Eggers spoke, and he realized that none of them had been approaching this mission with the right attitude.

The fact was that their approach had been fatalistic from the start… The odds seemed so badly stacked against them that none of them truly expected to survive, though not one of them had articulated their fears.

Apo grinned at Vicky, who looked just as astonished at Eggers' idea as everyone else. "I think now we will get a chance to rid the world of that *qaritukoq* Guzman forever." The word was Quechua for a man who pretends to be powerful when he is not, a poser.

"Apo, I want to do more than kill Guzman. I want to take him back to the States and humiliate him in front of the world," Vicky whispered. She liked and trusted Apo, but she could see in his eyes that he thought her desire was not punishment enough for Guzman's sins against the Quechua and certainly not repayment enough for what he had done to the children. She knew she was going to have to warn

Pete and Ving to keep an eye on the two Quechua men.

Brad sat eagerly scratching out the parts of his op order that needed to be changed and inserting the new information. The timetable for the assaults had just moved forward by several ideas, and he still needed to organize the aircraft loading and offloading plans, go over the approach routes, and conduct the test firing of the weapons. The work became suddenly much easier. Finally, they all felt hope, though their concerns about whether Delroy was still alive or not overshadowed their enthusiasm.

Chapter 12

Go!

In Flight

Day 3 1330 hours

Gunny Eggers planned to fly as co-pilot in the subdued Blackhawk helicopter that A & E Aviation had provided for the team's use. A & E kept the nondescript chopper to lease to clients, usually C.I.A. or U.S. military Special Operations, for use in clandestine ops.

The governments of Columbia, Venezuela, Peru, and Brazil also had need of their services for covert operations from time to time, and therefore A & E was able to operate the Blackhawk without the markings normally required by law. With the change in plans, the Blackhawk remained in its hangar back at the A & E compound at the airport.

Instead, Chief Eggers flew as pilot of the giant Chinook.

The big CH-47 with the A & E logo was a familiar sight all over the Amazon River Basin, constantly hired out to transport heavy equipment inside its spacious cargo compartment or slung beneath the chopper by steel cables suspended from the three ventral hooks on its underside. The big bird would not even be noticed in the late jungle afternoon.

An avionics technician installed the MAST before they took off from the compound at Francisco Secada Vignetta International Airport. It was fortunate that he was an accomplished technician because there had been damned little time to test the squad radios before they had to lift off. The system worked like a charm.

Eggers programmed the in-flight computer for Eureka, the first of the planned insertions. He, too, was caught up in the wave of hope shared by the team members ... and he felt now as if he had made a real contribution to the mission's chances of success.

Eureka

Brad knelt on the heavily vibrating cargo floor of the Chinook as it tilted back and flared towards the clear cut area beneath them. The tailgate was lowered, and Pete, Apo, and Jared stood clinging to the overhead steel cable that ran the length of the compartment. The three men were amped up, charged with the energy and sharpness that accompanied the anticipation of imminent combat.

"Remember, no matter what you find, don't open up until I give the word. I want us to hit all three locations at the same time," Brad said into the headset. All three tilted their heads in assent, but Pete and Jared knew Brad was telling them to keep an eye on Apo. Apo was fondling his M-60 with the familiarity of a '60 master anticipating being able to put the death-dealing weapon to its intended use.

The Chinook settled into a ground hover about four feet in the air and Brad yelled, "GO!"

Pete, out of long habit, ran three steps and fell to a prone position facing the direction of their planned route. Jared, second out of the chopper, did the same. Apo, his deeply tanned skin gleaming in the sun, lined the M-60 up along his side so its silhouette wouldn't be revealed. He remained standing, his eyes cast up to the blue sky as he said a final prayer to whatever deity he worshipped, asking for luck in finding Rodolfo Abimael Guzman so he could kill the bastard dead before Vicky could 'arrest' him and take him to the States.

The Chinook's nose tilted forward and the big helicopter moved north, picking up speed and altitude. Soon the huge clearing was quiet, and the sound of the Chinook was only faintly discernible.

Pete visually searched in a three hundred sixty degree pattern while Jared did the same. Apo completed his survey much more quickly, and before the other two men stood up, he jerked the bolt of the M-60 back and then let it slide forward, chambering a round. There appeared no sign of human activity other than themselves.

Pete decided to keep his mouth shut. Eggers had not reported any activity in the ground before he'd moved into his hover, and Pete had hit the ground out of habit. There was no sense making an issue of it, especially with a man who had grown up in these jungles. He made a 'come along' motion with his hand, and the three of them wordlessly moved into the jungle towards the Eureka compound three klicks (a klick is military slang for a thousand meters) away.

They moved out in single file. Pete didn't anticipate either booby traps or an ambush, but it made no sense to take chances. There were shallow graves the world over filled with the bones of men who didn't expect to encounter booby traps or ambushes.

Jared kept track of the pace, passing the word up to Pete when the count reached fifteen hundred meters. He saw Pete spread his arms to either side and both he and Apo spread out, their weapons all off safe.

The weight of the suppressed Sig Sauer Mosquito in its nylon holster against his hip was reassuring, and even the weight of the heavy Barrett .50 slung over his shoulder didn't bother him. The sniper rifle, or one identical to it, had become as natural a part of him as his arms or legs. He would have felt naked without it.

Pete held up a balled fist when they approached within a hundred meters of the grid coordinates the expats had given them. Jared began to wonder if they'd been sent on a wild goose chase, but Pete had spotted the reclining sentry, leaning against the trunk of a towering jacaranda and smoking a cheap cigarette.

Apo's sensitive nostrils had flared five minutes before, and he'd continued his silent movement through the jungle, wondering when Pete was going to see the sentry. He had known the man was there, he could smell the cigarette smoke. It had almost been necessary to tap the big man on the shoulder and call a halt when Pete signaled the presence of the sentry.

Apo quietly fell into a prone position and lay down his M-60 in preparation to advance on the sentry. The big Quechua grinned silently; he knew this was knife work. As he started to creep cautiously forwards he noticed Jared moving, and he froze. The man was moving in a way Apo had never seen a white man move before, it was like watching a ghost.

Even the insects and the snakes paid him no heed; it was almost as if Jared was indeed a spirit, haunting the day instead of the night. Apo shivered. For the first time, he realized he had badly underestimated these two Americans. They were not what he'd expected at all. He believed Vicky was an anomaly, and he had been wrong.

Jared had gotten within thirty feet of the sentry, moving like an avenging wraith. He settled down into a reinforced prone position in the jungle grass, took careful aim, and squeezed off two silent rounds. He was up and running in a silent crouch almost before the second round entered the sentry's left eye.

Reaching the tree, he lowered the sentry's AK-47 from its place against the tree trunk and placed it across the lap of the dead man and then made certain the body was not going to slump down. He then quickly returned to the spot where he dropped his M-16 and the Barrett and recovered them. Without a word, Pete rose and the three of them approached the compound.

When they got closer, it looked obvious that the Senderistas were not expecting company. Their weapons were stacked in the middle of the compound and the men were scattered around the compound, some eating, some chatting, a few snoozing, and a crowd of five played some kind of card game.

Pete signaled Apo to set up the M-60, and he and Jared dropped everything except the canvas bags that held the 'toys' Brad had obtained for them. Jared moved right and Pete moved left, concealing claymore mines at two places around the perimeter and observing the activity within the compound. Pete was the first one back to where Apo lay beneath some broad green leaves that resembled the elephant ear plants Pete's mother maintained at her home in Dallas.

Pete didn't dare speak into the headset for fear of alerting the Senderistas of their presence, so he tapped the throat mike of the radio headset and broke squelch once. Jared broke squelch twice in response, letting Pete know that he was alright and on his way back. The radio procedure was standard operating procedure for the team, but no one had thought to explain it to Apo. The big Quechua was savvy enough to hold his questions 'til later. So far, his two new friends appeared to know what they were doing and were surprisingly good at it.

When Jared returned, Apo was impressed even more. He didn't catch sight of the man until he was within ten feet of where the M-60 rested, and he never heard a sound as Jared crept up to lie alongside of him. Pete reached over and tapped Apo on the shoulder, then tapped Apo's headset, then mimed walking back away from the perimeter. Apo nodded his understanding, and then the two white men just seemed to evaporate. It occurred to the massive Mestizo that he was glad he was on their side. In minutes, Apo heard the two men whispering into his headset.

"You see any sign of Delroy or the kids, Jared?"

"No, I managed to get inside both the buildings, and the only one I found inside was one man with an AK. He won't be letting anyone know I visited ... ever."

"Shit! Nothing here at all?" Apo didn't hear a response from Jared. What he did hear was a click in his headset as Pete switched to the channel that permitted him to broadcast on both the squad channel and the command channel.

"Pete to Brad, over."

A moment passed before they heard Brad's voice. "Brad, over."

"No chicks in the nest," Pete whispered. "I say again, no chicks in the nest."

"Stand by," Brad said. The headsets went silent.

Nova Vida

Ving, Cauac, and Jessica encountered no problem after debarking the Chinook until they reached the Rio Javari. Jessica eyed the murky water skeptically, remembering what she knew of the indigenous wildlife, particularly the piranha, and she felt her skin crawl at the notion of swimming across the narrow river.

Cauac noticed her resistance and grinned at her. He pointed at a number of tangled vines with odd-shaped leaves dangling in the water. "You can swim safely wherever you see leaves like those in the water. Piranha hate them."

Relief washed over Jessica and she waded into the water and began to breaststroke her way across, holding her M-16 up out of the water.

Ving never hesitated, he waded straight into the water and swum across. He crawled up the slippery bank and into the woods beyond just as

Jessica dragged herself up. She turned to see Cauac reach one big hand down into the water and grab at his leg.

He scurried out of the water and Jess could see that he was slapping at a wriggling silver fish attached to the thick cloth of his jeans by a set of oversized teeth. There were three more of the struggling creatures flapping against his legs. In mounting horror, she realized they were piranha. She rushed to Cauac and slapped at the squirming fish until they fell to the ground and flopped their way back into the water.

"I thought you said they wouldn't attack when those leaves are in the water," she gasped.

Cauac gave her a broad grin. "If I hadn't told you that you'd still be on the other side of the river."

"You bastard!" she hissed.

Cauac didn't take offense. "It was easier than explaining that they usually don't attack unless they smell blood ... at least not in swarms the way they do when they kill. It's the snakes you have to watch out for."

Jessica was still incensed, but she was a trooper, and she turned and strode purposefully into the jungle. Cauac watched her admiringly for a moment and then followed her into the foliage, his M-60 at the ready.

Jessica didn't catch up to Ving until she had moved almost a hundred meters into the jungle. When she did catch him, Ving had one of the Senderistas in a half-nelson, one bear-like hand over the unfortunate man's mouth. With a mighty wrench, Ving broke the man's neck, the sound of the spine snapping much like the sound of someone stepping on a dry, brittle branch.

Ving, his face a mask of unconcern, lowered the body to the ground and lifted the Senderista's AK-

47. Calmly he broke the weapon open, extracted the bolt, and tossed it deep into the jungle. He quickly broke the weapon down, scattering parts all around. Jessica doubted anyone would ever be able to locate all the parts. Without saying a single word, Ving led the unit deeper into the jungle towards the only compound located in Brazil.

The approach to the compound was unguarded and very quiet, too quiet to suit Ving. When he reached a point he estimated to be about two hundred meters from the camp, he signaled to Jessica and Cauac to take up concealed defensive positions and slowly approached the camp as quietly as he could. Ving wasn't as stealthy as Jared, but he was close. His techniques for moving through forests had been developed at Parris Island and honed and refined over years of service in the Corps, much of it in combat.

Even focusing on stealth, Ving's mind was racing, evaluating what he knew of Jessica and Cauac's fieldcraft. So far, Cauac, the unknown quantity in the equation, had proven very adept at moving quietly in the jungle. That was to be expected because he had been raised in the Amazon Basin, but all he knew of the man's combat skills was what Vicky had related to him.

He possessed little to evaluate her experience either, other than that she said she had been in the Corps. He believed her, as much because Brad had as for any other reason. On the other hand, Brad *had* split Vicky and her two backups and put one in each assault unit.

Jessica remained solid, tough, and reliable, but Ving wasn't sure how well she could conduct a recon or, for that matter, how well she would be able to set the claymores.

When he reached the perimeter of the camp itself, his mind snapped back one hundred percent to the task at hand. He would conduct the recon himself, without the assistance of Jessica and the Quechua.

It might take a little longer, but he would be certain the effort had been thorough.

Jessica stared out through the jungle, wondering where Ving was and what was taking so long. She resisted the temptation to swat at the flies and mosquitos that plagued her, keeping still and limiting her head movements to slow, easy motions that allowed her to cover visually her half of the three hundred sixty degree perimeter she and Cauac were responsible for. She had learned that from Brad on their mission to Africa.

The sound of a single twig snapping caused her to move her head away from her assigned area of responsibility. When she did, she saw Cauac grinning at her and nodding in her direction. Her return smile froze on her face as she saw the Senderista sneaking up behind Cauac, his AK-47 aimed directly at the man's head.

She cursed silently as she realized that Ving was carrying the suppressed .22 Sig that Brad had given to the unit, and there was no time for her to do anything other than reach for the slender throwing knife she carried at her waist. She sat up and threw in the same fluid motion, and the silver blade flashed by a foot above Cauac's startled face. Jessica figured that even if the knife didn't stick it would distract the Senderista long enough for her to get to him.

She was wrong about the knife not sticking; it caught the approaching thug square in the throat, even as she closed the twenty-odd feet between them and wrestled his body to the ground. The Senderista stared into her eyes in total shock as he quivered once and then died. Cauac, stunned, at least maintained the good sense to remain quiet, nod his thanks to Jessica, and return his attention to his sector with renewed concentration.

The Senderista approached them from an oblique angle, out of an area that bisected their sectors of responsibility. He also gained a new respect for his attractive blonde partner. She looked every bit as deadly as Vicky. Cauac was definitely going to have to reconsider his opinion of pretty American women.

Ving, disgusted at having found no trace of his brother or the children, rigged his claymores. They were arranged in a line, close together to take advantage of the fact that the Senderistas were gathered around a fire, dining on the roasted carcass of some jungle animal and laughing and joking. If they remained still in place when Ving detonated the claymores, there wouldn't be much left of the group of twenty or so men.

He also managed to place most of his C-4 blocks to the back of the hut and the empty building where his brother or the children should have been held. Ving's grin was humorless as he crawled back to where he left Jessica and Cauac.

He was surprised and pleased to find the dead Senderista laid out behind Cauac, but he was even more surprised when he flashed a thumbs up sign to Cauac and the Mestizo shook his head no and pointed to Jessica. Jessica, once she verified that it was Ving approaching her position, never stopped the surveillance of her assigned area of responsibility. She was most definitely one of Brad's relatives. Ving felt a surge of pride as he reached up to key his throat mike.

Engano

Brad, Vicky, and Charlie stepped off the tailgate of the Chinook and hit the ground, staying prone until the Chinook began climbing up and to the left, heading towards the clear cut Eggers had found to wait for the signal to pick the units up. When they started to move, Brad let Vicky take point while a confused Charlie trailed behind them. Charlie appeared confused because he knew firsthand what an incredible tracker and navigator Brad was.

Brad was more interested in finding out what Vicky was made of. He let her take point after giving her a bearing and distance, while he kept a mental count of the pace.

Vicky's field craft turned out to be superlative. She moved through the jungle like a phantom, and she did it so fast that Brad was hard put to keep up with her. Her head was in constant motion, missing nothing. Her feet set down silently and surely, avoiding everything that might crackle or snap beneath them. In short, he was thoroughly impressed. She seemed every bit as good as Jared, and Jared was one of the very best.

Vicky stopped them with a raised fist when they were still two hundred meters from their objective by Brad's calculations. Brad and Charlie sank to one knee, but Vicky signaled them to go prone, and quickly. They complied immediately. Brad started to low crawl towards her, but she stayed him with a hand movement that exposed her palm to him.

He still did not see what had prompted her halting them, but as he watched she began to wriggle forward on her belly.

Vicky literally slithered like one of the native reptiles, and then she simply vanished from his sight. Alarmed, Brad motioned Charlie to follow him, and the two men crawled forward as swiftly as they could without giving away their positions.

When they reached the spot where Vicky had disappeared, Brad was surprised to find her crouched over the form of a Senderista sentry, searching his clothing for weapons. The man appeared unconscious, but he was breathing. Vicky produced a set of handcuffs from somewhere and she gagged him with a bandana from her pocket.

She glared at Brad when she saw him, but she kept working, trussing the sentry up so firmly he would be unable to get out of his bonds. If for any reason they didn't manage to get back to him the guy was as good as dead.

With hand motions Vicky let him know that the sentry carried no papers, maps or weapons on him... He was of no further use to them at the moment. Brad debated putting a round from the suppressed .22 in his head, but Vicky shook her head no and began to move again.

Brad glanced back at Charlie, who shrugged and got to his feet. He turned back to see Vicky disappearing into the foliage ahead and then got to his own feet and moved out after her. She wanted the sentry alive; that much was clear. Brad hoped like hell he could remember how to find the man again, otherwise the jungle creatures would be eating better than nature intended as soon as it got dark. However rotten the poor bastard was, he didn't deserve to be eaten alive by one of the big jungle cats. Just the thought of that gave Brad the shivers.

They had moved forward only about fifty more meters when Vicky came back and gave them the sign to designate the objective rally point, the point they would return to if things went bad at the objective. In civilian terms, it was the closest they could get to the camp and still be able to whisper to each other without being detected. It didn't really matter; the headsets they were using enabled them to speak in a sub-whisper that was inaudible from a couple of feet away.

She came close and knelt down in front of them, speaking with as few words as possible.

"Fifty meters … compound occupied … sentries ahead, one left, and one right." Her eyes were wide with excitement. "Prisoners! Kids and Delroy!"

Brad felt exultation flood through him! Vicky had been in Peru before, and she would have recognized Delroy from the photos Ving showed her of his baby brother. He raised his eyebrows in a silent question.

"Looks rough, but alive." Vicky touched the claymore bags draped over Brad's shoulder and looked at him expectantly. She obviously wanted to know how he intended to deploy the claymores since the prisoners were present.

"Let me think," Brad whispered.

At that moment the three of them heard a single click over the air. It was Pete, reporting that there were no prisoners. Brad had just told him to stand by when he heard Ving's voice chime in over the air.

"None here either, over." There was barely concealed fury and anxiety both in Ving's voice.

"I have the chicks here; I say again, chicks here. Over."

"Don't start the party without us, over." Ving's exultation was fierce, and, despite his obvious effort, he couldn't disguise it.

The idea and the decision came easily, and Brad didn't hesitate. "Pete, Ving, have you deployed your toys? Over."

"Roger that! Over," Pete said.

"Ditto! Over," Ving said. Brad could tell Ving was anticipating his next command; they had been through too much together for his friend not to know his mind.

"Give me ten mikes to get birdman aloft and pull the plug on those toys. I say again, pull the chain! Birdman will pick you up to bring you here ASAP. Copy?"

"Roger, copy! Out."

Ving's voice came back cool and calm, though Brad knew what it cost his friend in effort to suppress his joy. "Roger, pull the chain in ten mikes. Out."

"Birdman, how copy, over?"

"Birdman copies, winding up the rubber bands now. Airborne in ten mikes, en route to extract unit one and transport to unit three location. Birdman out." Eggers was already firing up the two massive Lycoming engines on the Chinook. Brad could hear the whine of the starters over the headset.

'Pull the chain' is a phrase used by military units when they are being overrun by the enemy and they are requesting that their own artillery fire an intense barrage on their own position. It is a desperation plea designed to destroy the enemy, even if it means the friendly forces don't survive.

When used in the circumstances Brad was using it in, it was a command to inflict maximum casualties on and to obliterate the enemy. He wanted the Senderistas rendered harmless as quickly and ruthlessly as possible. He also wanted the other two camps in panic mode in the hopes that Guzman and his minions would learn of the attacks and be stirred up—agitated people make mistakes.

Brad turned his mind to the Engano camp and the most effective places to use the demolitions he had on hand. He would protect the kids at all costs, and Delroy, too, but suddenly he had an urge, an urge to wipe out this branch of the Shining Path movement as an object lesson to others who would sell children into sexual slavery. He had reached the limit of his patience. If it didn't work, it didn't work, but in the final analysis, some things were worth risking your life for.

Chapter 13

The Final Assault

Phase I

Pete's face lit up with excitement when he switched back to the 'unit only' channel and addressed Apo and Jared. "You guys ready?" he asked eagerly. He directed Apo to an area twenty meters outside the compound's barbed wire fence, one that had the best field of fire for the M-60.

Apo sought his eyes and Pete responded to his unasked question. "Get as many as you can, brother. Brad wants them to get the message out to Guzman, but what the hell? There's three of us and twenty of them. We'll worry about causing panic later."

Pete nodded to Jared. He'd known the rangy Texan for years and he knew the man's abilities. Jared would find the best spot from which to ply his

243

trade. He remained the best sniper Pete had ever seen. "The big boom is the signal to give 'em hell, guys."

Pete double-checked to ensure that neither Apo nor Jared was in the backblast area of the claymores he set up before connecting the clackers to the end of the detonator wires. From his prone position, he watched the movement in the compound, trying to make certain as many of the Senderistas stayed in the path of the claymore's blast zone as possible before detonating the first mine. Pete checked his watch. Four more minutes.

Jared found a vantage point in the broad, thick branches of a tree he didn't recognize, and he climbed up to make sure he'd still have good fields of fire into the compound. The branch he selected ended up being even wider than he'd imagined, and he was able to take a good prone position with the Barrett.

He focused the adjustable ranging Redfield scope, trusting that the bore sighting whoever prepped the big rifle had done was accurate. It really wouldn't matter, at this range he could use the quick-disconnect and use the iron sights if necessary. After scoping the group and trying to determine which of Guzman's thugs was the leader and failing to single one out, Jared removed the scope.

Jared and Apo were startled when a jubilant Pete screamed, "Hey guys!" at the top of his lungs. The Senderistas appeared shocked as well, and they turned to face the direction from which the shout had come. It was their last mistake. The massive roar of the first claymore's detonation was quickly followed by a second, and Jared punched the button for the radio detonation device hooked to his two mines.

Few of the Senderistas were left standing after the smoke cleared. Jared took out one man stumbling about, his hands covering the bloody mess that had been his face a moment before. The roar of the M-60 cutting loose off to his left drew his attention, and Jared turned his head to see Apo firing the weapon from the hip, a feat most men couldn't manage.

Vicky had been right; the big Quechua was an artist with the machine gun. Pete was watching as well, his mouth open in surprise. The smoke and falling debris had not yet settled from the explosions before Apo lowered the smoking barrel of the M-60. The massively muscled man surveyed his work for a moment and turned away from the carnage. He was smiling as he began to walk rapidly through the jungle, following the same trail they had used coming in.

"Come on, boss man," he called over his shoulders. "We don't want to be late for the next round. Rodolfo is waiting…"

With a wry grin, Pete dropped the clackers in his hand and followed him. Jared shinnied down his tree, collecting a few splinters along the way, and then jogged over to catch up with Pete.

"She was right," Jared said.

"What?" Pete asked.

"He's a freakin' artist with a '60."

Minutes later, the Chinook tilted forward and rose into the sky. Pete, Jared, and Apo were sitting in the collapsible canvas seats on either side of the cargo compartment, wiping down their weapons.

"Birdman to Brad. Unit one collected and in the air! Birdman out."

Phase II

Ving watched as the second hand on his chronograph swept towards the ten-minute mark, the single clacker in his hand wired to all four claymores. There remained still more than a minute to go before he was supposed to set them off.

It was Jessica who spotted the guys who screwed up the plan. Four men approached the stronghold on foot through the jungle from the direction of the river. Ving was so focused on the compound that he didn't notice them, and apparently so was Cauac.

When Jessica noticed them, they were less than twenty feet behind Cauac, and she involuntarily screamed his name before sitting up from her prone covered position just before she opened up on the men with her M-16. Her shout alerted the men around the fire, who immediately dispersed, running for their stacked weapons and taking many of them out of the blast area of Ving's claymores.

Cauac spun in his position, swinging the twenty-three-pound M-60 as if it were no heavier than a broomstick. Jessica had already taken out the lead Senderista when Cauac's M-60 barked its death song, but her actions cost her.

Ving had turned to see the oncoming Senderistas when Jessica yelled and jumped up to shoot at them. He was still screaming at her to lie back down when a hail of bullets came from the compound, where the bulk of the Senderistas had figured out they were under attack. Ving roared as he saw Jessica fall in a hail of gunfire, and he triggered the claymores in his rage. Cauac spun again, raking the Senderistas with automatic fire.

Ving dropped the clacker, the blast from the simultaneous detonations of the claymores still ringing in his ears, and ran towards where Jessica lay writhing in the deep grass and clutching at her thigh. "Go," she gasped when he reached her. "I'll be okay; it just hurts like a bitch! Go! Kill those bastards!"

Ving stared at her for a moment before coming back to reality. Then his wrath returned, and he fell on the Senderistas like an avenging angel. The two men waded through the wounded Senderistas in an orgy of bloodlust, in their minds they were avenging the rape of children and there was no appeasing them.

When it was over and silence reigned, Ving was crying, something he hadn't done since his mother had died. When he was satisfied that they were all dead, he returned to where Cauac was binding Jessica's thigh with cellophane that had apparently covered a portion of the food the Senderistas had brought with them.

"Jesus Cauac, there's no telling what kind of germs are on that piece of garbage!"

Cauac looked up at him solemnly. "Whatever is on it, boss, is bound to be better than the parasites in the Rio Javari."

Ving, stunned, had forgotten that they had to cross the damned river—and that the river contained piranha that would go berserk at the scent of blood in the water. He waited until Cauac finished, and then he bent down and lifted Jessica in his arms.

"I can walk, Ving," Jessica said disgustedly.

"The hell you can," Ving said pleasantly. "Get as much of her stuff as you can carry, Cauac. You're going to have to help me when we get to the river. We can't let that leg get in the water."

"That's why I wrapped it in plastic," Cauac observed.

"Yeah, but we don't know how much is in her clothes," Ving responded. "And I have no desire to be eaten alive by your little fish buddies."

Ving walked as if Jessica's weight was no greater than a bag of chewing tobacco, and they reached the river just as they heard the sound of the

Chinook landing in the clear cut just a hundred yards away.

They were halfway across the river when Pete, Apo, and Jared appeared on the opposite bank. Between the five of them they managed to get Jessica out of the river and back to the Chinook.

"Birdman to Brad. Unit two collected and in the air! Birdman out."

Phase III

Eggers set the Chinook down in the LZ near Engano, and he jumped back in the cargo area even before the giant rotors stopped.

"What the hell are you doing, Chief?" Ving demanded.

"I'm going with you," the older man said, stone faced. "I heard Brad talking to his team on the radio... He forgot to switch back from the command channel a while ago. You guys are facing some pretty stiff odds here, not just twenty or thirty shooters, and, besides, the kids are here.

"You've got your bone to pick with them, Ving, 'cause they got your brother. I've got my own bone to pick with 'em." His face looked red with anger. He was furious over the treatment of the kids; he had three granddaughters of his own back in the States. Nobody was going to talk him out of going on this little hunt.

Jessica was proving to be just as difficult. She was standing up in the troop compartment, and it appeared obvious that she was in pain. It was just as obvious that she was determined to go to the fight. "I'm going, Ving, and you can't stop me. Of course it hurts, it hurts like hell, but I can stand on it and I'm going—period."

Ving recognized the look on her face; it was one she'd inherited from the same place Brad had gotten his. Her beloved cousin, her lover, and her closest friends would soon be at the sharp point of the sword and she would not be denied. Ving shrugged. Brad would give him hell, but Jessica was correct. She had a right.

They poured off the chopper together, racing as fast as Jessica's leg would allow them to travel. Two hundred meters down the faint track they heard the distinct sound of an M-60 opening up. This time Apo picked Jessica up and threw her over his shoulder despite her objections.

With the white girl over his shoulder and the M-60 dangling from his huge hand, he began to sprint towards the sound of gunfire. The rest of them spread out, weapons at the ready, and ran towards the camp and the final confrontation with Rodolfo Abimael Guzman. The time of reckoning had come.

The Reckoning

Brad crawled to a spot where he could keep an eye on the compound as he waited for the arrival of the rest of his team. He had placed Charlie on a slight elevation that gave him a decent field of fire with his M-249, but Brad wasn't convinced the man could handle the weapon as well as he would need him to. Now that he could see just how many men Guzman had with him, he was more than a little glad that things had worked out as they had.

Attacking forty or more armed men with just the three of them would have been near suicidal, especially with a question mark for a gunner. If it came down to a pitched battle before Ving and the others showed up, he would probably take the M-249 from Charlie and use it himself. The odds were too stacked against them.

It wasn't that he doubted that Charlie would fight, he knew better than to worry about that. The problem was that there were kids in the compound and he knew Charlie had never done more than familiarization firing with the M-249. They hadn't come all this way to kill Delroy and the kids by accident.

Vicky, impatient to find out what was going on, had low crawled up to where he was and settled into the heavy grass next to him. Brad refused to be distracted, and he kept his eyes shifting over the Senderistas. The bastards had brought Delroy out of the larger of the huts just a few minutes earlier, and Guzman himself appeared standing in front of the kneeling American, berating him loudly before the assembled Senderistas.

Delroy bore the abuse in silence, and Guzman raised his hand to strike the kneeling man. Just as Guzman was about to unleash a blow to Delroy's head, the signature sound of the Chinook landing reverberated through the jungle. Guzman stopped with his arm drawn back and stared in the direction of the chopper's landing. He began to scream in Quechua, pointing towards the sound of the Chinook's dying engines.

"Oh hell," Vicky said, getting to her knees.

"Get down!" Brad hissed. Vicky was lifting her M-16 as Guzman was lowering his hand to his hip to draw a rather large and menacing looking pistol.

"He's just told his men to go to meet the chopper... They never stop here and he's sure it's us. Brad, he's going to shoot your friend!" The fifty or sixty-odd men in the compound scattered, picking up their weapons, and began to run towards the gate.

"Shit!" Brad exclaimed as Vicky squeezed off a round, striking Guzman in the shoulder. It would have been a head shot if the man hadn't suddenly bent forward to place the barrel of his pistol against Delroy's head.

Brad ran to where Charlie was frantically trying to ram a round into the chamber. He grabbed the weapon and dropped his M-16 beside Charlie. He turned around, yanking the bolt back and letting it slam home after ejecting the bent round from the chamber. Squeezing the trigger, sending three to six round bursts into the charging Senderistas, Brad strode towards the compound.

Before he had taken three steps, some of Guzman's men had taken cover and were returning his fire. Bullets whined past his ear and whipped through the tall grass around him.

"Brad! Look out!" Vicky yelled as she ran towards him. He watched her fall, knocked forward onto her face by the force of a 7.62 round fired from an AK-47. Brad felt a sinking feeling as he watched her crumple up on the ground and lie still. The sinking feeling turned to ice, he was convinced she was dead, but the bullets around him were thicker now, and he was suddenly fighting for his life. He dropped to a prone position and began selecting his targets.

The Senderistas finally got a crew served machine gun working, and a withering hail of bullets chewed up the jungle. Brad swiftly switched his radio onto the command channel and yelled something incomprehensible into it.

"We're here, Brad!" Ving's voice called over the radio, and Brad watched in relief as Cauac and Ving stepped out of the jungle nearly forty meters to his right. Jared and Pete were firing from either side of the two huge men, and a split second later Apo opened up with his M-60 from a position just a few yards to Brad's right, between him and Charlie.

"Careful, don't hit the kids! Watch the kids!" Brad screamed into his headset. The crew served machine gun swung around to engage Pete and Cauac, and Brad saw Cauac go down and Pete falter under the deadly hail of flying lead. Apo shifted his fire to the sandbagged machine gun position, forcing the gunner and his assistant to duck down behind the sandbags.

Jessica stumbled up beside Brad and fell to the ground beside him. He wanted to ask her if she was hit, but she began methodically firing into the compound, selecting her targets carefully and taking out Senderistas with frighteningly accurate fire. Suppressing a surge of pride, Brad scanned the encampment, looking for Guzman.

He noted that Delroy was on the ground, wriggling his way towards the hut where most of the children were being held. He continued yelling something at them, but Brad couldn't make out what he kept saying over the sound of the gunfire.

Brad had been unable to deploy his claymores because he had been afraid of hurting the kids, and he remained much too far out to toss his grenades.

Apo's M-60 stopped chattering as he jerked open the feed tray and racked the bolt to the rear to insert another bandolier of linked ammo. The gunner and assistant gunner at the crew served gun swung the barrel of their weapon around to bear on the huge Quechua, but as their heads popped up, the Barret roared twice, and the two heads disappeared in geysers of blood and bone.

The firing slowed as the number of Senderistas diminished. Soon there was only scattered resistance, and then the compound fell silent.

"Sit-rep, sound off!" Brad spoke into his headset.

"I'm good," Jared answered.

"I'm hit, Brad, but I can walk." Brad was relieved, he had seen Pete get hit, and he'd thought his friend had bought it.

"I'm okay," Apo said, looking around him. He was dripping blood from a small caliber bullet that had struck him in the thigh, but it didn't seem to hinder him in the least. "Where's Cauac? Anybody see Cauac?"

"Over here," Pete said quietly. Cauac was never going to talk on a squad radio again. His chest was riddled with bullet holes and he lay bent over his M-60, his arms splayed out in death.

"I'm alright," Jessica said. "Oh crap, Brad, Vicky's moving!" Jess scrambled over to the slim redhead and felt under her shirt where dark red blood was spreading. The bullet had missed her lung by mere millimeters, but the force of the round had slammed her to the ground. She had hit her head on a log and been rendered unconscious.

"Owww, dammit that hurts," Vicky groaned. She looked up at Brad. "Casualties?" she asked.

"Just about everybody," Brad said grimly as he knelt beside her with a field pressure dressing. He unbuttoned her blouse and shoved her bra aside before putting the compress on the wound and pressing down to stanch the unusually small flow of blood.

"It went in through my back," Vicky said.

"Through and through," Brad said, "I guess that's why there's so little blood."

Vicky groaned again as she lifted her head. "Did we lose anyone?"

Brad nodded. "Cauac."

"Oh God!" Vicky choked back the sob that came to her throat. She had known Cauac and Apo for a long time, and she'd liked the big man. "Where's Apo?"

"He's with Cauac. I think he caught a round, too, but he's not even limping."

Jessica was limping inside the compound, leaning against Charlie and accompanied by Ving, Jared, and Eggers. Despite Ving's eagerness to find out if Delroy was okay, he kept moving slowly through the bodies. Apo caught up with them and started kicking at the bodies to make certain they were dead. His face looked impassive, but he carried one of the .45s tightly in one massive fist. It looked like a toy in his hand.

"Delroy!" Ving called out.

"I knew you'd come after me, Mason!" Delroy staggered out the door of the hut. He dropped to his knees, blood pouring from wounds in his torso. Ving rushed to his aid, but Delroy waved him off. "The kids, Mason, check the kids first. I'm okay." He slumped forward into Ving's arms.

"We'll check on the kids, Ving," Jessica said, limping towards the hut. "You go ahead and help your brother."

Charlie opened the door of the hut, and Jessica prepared for a rush of frightened children, but she was stunned at what she saw. There were roughly thirty children inside the hut, huddled together and shivering with fear. They were afraid to come to her.

Tears filled her eyes as she read the stark terror in their eyes. "What's wrong with them?" she sobbed. "Why won't they come to me?" She stared at them.

They all appeared unhurt and well fed, and they were relatively clean. "They don't look as if they've been mistreated."

One of the older girls, perhaps twelve or so, screwed up her face and walked up to Charlie. With a shrug of her shoulders, she slipped her simple cotton shift off and lay down on the dirt floor with her legs spread wide. Her eyes were tightly closed.

In a choked voice, Charlie explained as he knelt by the little girl and gently encouraged her to put her dress back on. "They won't have any visible marks. That would take away from their value on the auction blocks. The marks and scars they carry are on the inside." His voice broke as the little girl stared back at him, confused.

"What was she doing, Charlie? Why did she do that?"

Charlie was crying unashamedly. "She was offering herself to me so that I wouldn't take one of the younger ones," he whispered.

The rage blew up inside Jessica like a summer thunderstorm, black as sin and expanding like an explosion. She turned and stalked out of the hut. She wanted to scream. Instead, she turned and stalked into the other hut, the one she had seen Guzman come out of when they brought Delroy outside. The hut was divided into four rooms.

She found Guzman in the last room by following a blood trail from the front door. The monster had been hit with several bullets in the fleshy parts of his body, but at least one had struck his spine. He was whining and crying as his fingers scrabbled with the latch on a trap door in the floor.

Despite the pain of her injury, Jessica bent over and grabbed the crippled leader of the Shining Path movement in Iquitos by the shoulders. He cried out in pain and begged her not to kill him in English. He begged for mercy.

"Mercy?" she raged. "The same kind of mercy you showed to those kids out there?" Her out flung arm pointed towards the hut where her lover sat trying to convince the children that their ordeal was finally over.

Guzman's bravado was all used up. He blubbered and squalled, still begging for mercy from this blonde avenging angel from hell. He even had the nerve to start praying.

Jessica's rage boiled over. She turned him over onto his back, ignoring his screams of pain. Then she crossed his feet at the ankles. She almost lost her nerve and her rage when she heard the bones in his spine grind against each other when she rearranged his legs, accompanying his shrieks of agony. Jessica tied his hands with his own bootlaces, and then she stood up.

"You're a fucking monster! If you live through this, which I seriously doubt, you will never molest another child, I can promise you that." Her face set in stone, she reached in one of the cargo pockets of her pants and brought out a cylindrical object. It was OD green, and the legend "Smoke, WP, Burst type" was clearly legible on the front.

Deliberately, she pulled the pin on the incendiary grenade and tucked it down the front of his trousers until it rested on the physiological manifestation of his gender. She then released the handle and quickly removed her hand from inside his baggy white pants. She rubbed her hand disgustedly on the seat of her pants. "I'd tell you to burn in hell," she said, "but I think you're going to feel the flames long before you get there." The front of his pants began to smolder, and Guzman's screams got louder.

Jessica turned and left the room without saying another word. Guzman screamed for a long time, but he stopped well before the hut caught fire and burned to the ground. Nobody asked her what she had done.

Chapter 14

Cabo Again

Epilogue

"Ow!" Vicky said, "Take it easy! That's still tender."

Brad smiled down at her, his hands uncommonly gentle as he rubbed the sunscreen on the skin above her swelling breasts. "Sorry," he said.

"You are not!" Vicky teased. "You just enjoy taking liberties with my body." She reached out with the hand on her uninjured side and caught his hand in hers.

"You never complained before," he responded with a grin, squeezing her hand.

"That was before some clown put a bullet in my back," she protested. "You didn't spend nearly as much time on my back as you did with this one on my chest!"

"That's an entrance wound," Brad said, "and, besides, this side is more interesting."

Vicky glanced over at the side of the pool, where Charlie sat performing a similar task for Jessica. To either side of the couple were the rest of the team's walking wounded. A nurse from the resort staff was performing a similar service for Ving, and Pete lay staring wistfully at the attractive woman's derriere.

"I wish I had a picture of this I could take back to show Willona!" Pete exclaimed.

Jared, who escaped unscathed, laughed delightedly and took a picture with his cell phone. "What am I bid for this picture? Highest bidder gets it."

Ving sighed and grinned. "You schmucks wouldn't know what to do with a real woman if you had one," he taunted.

The team's shared laughter was cathartic, freeing them from the horrors they had seen over the previous few days and purging their souls. They were closer than they had ever been. Jessica had silently assumed the status of a full-fledged member of the team. She was no longer a young adventuress; she had finally won her spurs as a warrior. The others accepted her as one of them, even Brad, who loved her because she was his devoted cousin who had looked up to him from her childhood.

There was another on the threshold of acceptance, waiting only on her expression of willingness to be one of them. Vicky had demonstrated beyond a shadow of a doubt that she was worthy of the title Warrior, but she was an active special agent for I.C.E. It remained to be seen whether she would be willing to join their ranks ... and whether Brad would ask her since he was obviously smitten with her.

Vicky sensed that he wanted to ask her, but she knew he had mixed feelings about taking her into the kinds of situations that his team specialized in. She had mixed feelings as well but not about the action. Despite the horrors she had seen and the aching loss of a trusted friend, she wouldn't shy away from combat. She had to admit she was something of an adrenaline junkie, and Brad's team promised to fulfill that need in her psyche.

What she feared was letting down the uncounted thousands of stolen kids, kids forced to live as sexual slaves for perverted rich men who lived and played in foreign countries that maintained unfavorable extradition laws. The reason she was even considering an invitation from Brad to join his team was the fact that they didn't have their hands tied by a bureaucracy that restricted them to the letter of the law and be damned to the intent. It was not a decision she wanted to make without considerable thought—clear, untainted thought.

For that, she was going to have to say goodbye to Brad for a while, put some space between them, because he made her senses swim and her body sing. For the moment, she was content just to enjoy him.

Brad surveyed his team, feeling a justifiable pride in their skill and the sense of family they shared. He knew there was not a better combination of personnel in all the world and he had worked with some of the best. His mind turned to the op they just finished. It had been yet another one for which he had not been paid and it depleted his war chest considerably. He managed to extricate them all before the authorities had gotten wind of what they had done, and he felt no remorse or guilt over the mission.

They had rid the world of an evil man who was willing to do the unspeakable for a price, and he would not be missed. There would be another to take his place, Brad had no doubt, but the next one would be aware that his actions might not be tolerated, that there remained forces at large in the world that were willing to do what was necessary just because it was the right thing to do. For Brad, that was enough. The money didn't matter at all.

THE END.

Thank you for taking the time to read TRACK DOWN AMAZON. If you enjoyed it, please consider telling your friends or posting a short review. Word of mouth is an author's best friend and much appreciated. Thank you, Scott Conrad.

EXCLUSIVE SNEAK PEAK – TRACK DOWN IRAQ – BOOK 4

He prayed that his death would be quick and violent instead of slow and painful. The black robed DAESH troops were particularly brutal towards the mercenaries when they captured them. He had seen the brutality firsthand, and it was not pretty.

Brandon Murphy, or "Murph", as he was known by his friends, squatted in a dark corner in an alleyway in the Al-Tameem neighborhood of Mosul, Iraq. As he fought to catch his breath, he wiped the dust from his face with the tail of his ragged, black-and-white checkered keffiyeh. The keffiyeh was de rigueur for locals, and it concealed

Murph's decidedly European features from the militants as well as from the Shia militiamen supporting the Iraqi troops.

Murph and five other Belus security contractors were the only members left of the support team Belus had committed to Iraq's Golden Division ... elite U.S. Special Forces trained Special Operations troops of the Iraqi Army.

Belus was a huge private military company with close ties to the Iraqi government, and had been hired by the State Department as "advisors" to Iraqi Special Ops. Murph and a platoon of Belus security contractors had been embedded with the Golden Division just prior to the November 1 dawn commencement of Operation "We Are Coming, Nineveh." Within hours of the onset of hostilities, all pretense of Murph's status as trainer and adviser had been abandoned, and the platoon was spread over the entire division in groups of six.

Special Operations leaders detailed them to problem areas, where Murph and his companions resolved particularly thorny situations enabling their Iraqi counterparts to continue with their missions. By the third day they operated mostly independently, though they received instructions via radio. By the time they reached the Al-Tameem neighborhood of Mosul, they were so far separated from the Golden Division troops that they were having trouble getting resupplied.

They had long since been forced to replenish their ammunition, ordnance and other supplies from the bodies of DAESH insurgents. They accepted what food and water they could get from citizens who refused to abandon their homes because of the fighting. Batteries for their radios were not available, and the one Murph carried, he'd resorted to turning it on for only moments at a time. The battery was so close to dead he had no idea if his transmissions were getting out ... he sure as hell wasn't getting much in the way of radio traffic.

He no longer knew if any friendlies knew where the hell they were, or even if anybody cared. He was also having a hell of a time telling who was friendly and who was not. Even the Golden Division troops were not all in a common uniform. Many of the players in this damned war looked pretty much the same, and the Iraqi regulars had abandoned so much equipment when Mosul fell in June of 2014 that they were driving Humvees and carrying M-16s and CAR-4s.

A burst of automatic weapons fire erupted at the end of the alley ...

A Brad Jacobs Thriller Series by Scott Conrad:

TRACK DOWN AFRICA – BOOK 1

TRACK DOWN ALASKA – BOOK 2

TRACK DOWN AMAZON – BOOK 3

TRACK DOWN IRAQ – BOOK 4

TRACK DOWN BORNEO – BOOK 5

TRACK DOWN EL SALVADOR – BOOK 6

TRACK DOWN WYOMING – BOOK 7

Visit the author at: ScottConradBooks.com

Printed in Great Britain
by Amazon